A REVIEWER'S GUIDE TO WRITING BOOK REVIEWS

AND HOW TO GET PAID FOR THEM

RICK HIPSON

Let the world know:
#IGotMyCLPBook!

Crystal Lake Publishing
www.CrystalLakePub.com

WELCOME
TO ANOTHER

CRYSTAL LAKE PUBLISHING
CREATION

Join today at www.crystallakepub.com & www.patreon.com/CLP

TABLE OF CONTENTS

GRATITUDE

Special thanks to Marie-France Brunet, Chris Carelse, Jacinta Williams, Scott Light, and Grant Anthony, my early readers, for their invaluable eyeballs and insight.

Thank you to RC Matheson, Barry Hoffman, Joe Mynhardt, and Candace Nola for classing up the joint with your experienced insight into why reviews matter.

All you wonderful humans helped make this book better.

Thanks to every author and publisher who trusted me with their work over the past 20(!) years. You are legion and too numerous to list here, but I trust you know who you are.

An extra special thanks to Monica S. Kuebler, author and veteran book editor for Rue Morgue magazine. Thanks for working with me over the years and making me a better reviewer. Glad I cornered you that one drunken night.

Thanks to Joe Mynhardt of Crystal Lake Publishing for allowing me to join your stellar family. I am immensely grateful to say the very least.

An extra special thanks to my partner in life, Jessie Tunney. You make all this worth it.

And, of course, thanks to YOU! Yeah you, the one reading this and the reason for this guide. May it serve you well and help spread the love of books we all share.

Thank you all.

FOREWORD

BEFORE WE BEGIN, let's get something out of the way: books about writing are weird. That's not to say that there aren't some amazing, life-changing ones, but when—at least to me—so much of the writing process feels like sitting down at a desk and harnessing some strange otherworldly primordial force, how do you teach that? Everyone throws different things into their literary cauldron in a different order to cast their spell. It's basically alchemy, the kind from the Middle Ages when it was believed lead could be made into gold. Except with writing, it works. Writing can be transformative.

Of course, they also teach it in schools, so it can't be *that* magic, and a lot of writing, like feature writing or reviewing, comes with a set of hard and fast rules and best practices. In the days before the internet—this is where I admit I'm more or less a dinosaur—if you didn't go to school for writing and wanted to break into entertainment journalism, you'd cut your teeth publishing your work in local zines for free until you could convince an editor at some established publication that you had enough talent or sheer stick-with-it-ness to give you a chance and teach you everything the amateurs at the zines couldn't. Then maybe, someday, after writing many, many, *many* reviews and other things, you might be lucky enough to become one of those editors yourself, as I have. And it all started with a passion for horror fiction—and penning reviews.

Reviewing is different things to different people, for some it's a vehicle to more substantial assignments, while others see it as an endgame in and of itself. For me, reviewing has always been an adventure, especially in the years before I could choose my own assignments. Sure, there were many mediocre, forgettable novels (all still deserving of fair, well-reasoned reviews), but there were

i

also books so mind-blowing that they inspired me to immediately devour a writer's entire back catalogue, and what a thrill to rave about such a book in a magazine and turn fellow horror fans onto its dark delights or a new favourite author. It's always flattering when someone thanks me for all the amazing books they have discovered through my reviews.

Yet, when Rick approached me to write a foreword to his book, I was surprised. Yes, I also got my start reviewing, but why on earth would he want his notoriously hard-ass, super nitpicky editor to do this? Didn't he know what he was getting himself into? He was just as likely to get notes on the book's content in addition to a foreword. Never mind that whole "I find books about writing weird" thing.

From the outset, it was clear we weren't going to agree on everything. For instance, Rick speaks candidly about how he views his role as a reviewer as supporting authors and publishers first and foremost, but as his editor at *Rue Morgue*, I'd argue that our first responsibility is to the magazine's readership. Is this release something they should spend their hard-earned money on—why or why not? Our publication exists in part to help them make an educated decision. Regular readers get to know a reviewer's tastes and come to trust them. It's a good thing then that Rick follows that up with a section on the importance of honesty in reviewing, and how to back up thoughts and feelings with examples from the material, so at least we won't have to duke it out in the ring.

After reading *A Reviewer's Guide to Writing Book Reviews and How to Get Paid For Them*, I think I know why he asked me, and it wasn't so I could give him a hard time in the introduction. It's because I can see this book for what it is: a short cut. A step up. A way to slip closer to the front of the would-be writer line. It's a gift.

If you read closely and follow Rick's advice (even if only the parts that speak to you), there's a great deal of useful information to be found within, especially for those just dipping their toes in and sampling the water. He touches on all the crucial stuff, from the importance of having a passion for the subject matter *and* the craft of reviewing; to the style, content, and structure of book reviews; to best practices for approaching and communicating with authors and publishers; and even the different places, traditional and otherwise, where a review—amateur or professional—might find a home.

FOREWORD

While Rick may not devote a lot of the book's real estate to the qualities that make him a valuable member of *Rue Morgue*'s stable of writers, they're well worth highlighting here. Namely, graciousness and expediency when receiving editorial notes and rewrite requests; sending in timely, well-researched pitches; a tireless enthusiasm to hone his craft; and a slavish dedication to meeting deadlines. (Confession: Editors love reviewers who can make a deadline. It's fucking hot.) A writer can be wildly talented and that will open doors, but it's the ones who are professional, eager, and make their editors' lives easier that land the most assignments.

I know this. Rick knows this. And if you read this book, you'll also know this (as well as many other things), and you'll be well on your way to writing—and maybe even selling—your first review. Good luck! I can't wait to see your pitches in my inbox.

Monica S. Kuebler
Toronto, Canada
April 2024

WHO THE HELL AM I AND HOW DID I GET HERE?

BEFORE YOU START asking, "Who the hell are you, and what makes you think you know it all?" (that's what I'd be asking), let me get a few things out of the way.

First, when it comes to reviewing books, I don't know it all, not by a long shot. I doubt anyone does, and I'm certain there are many who know a lot more than I do; that you can bet on. I know what I know, and that's all that I know. Besides, I wouldn't need so many books about writing on my shelves if I already knew it all. I learned something from each of them because not everyone has the same perspective, approach, style, or experience. That's what I hope you get from this guide: a little something different you might not have collected elsewhere, something based on my personal experience, style, approach, and perspective. And if you happen to learn something new, be sure to put it in your toolbox with all the other tools you've picked up along the way from other writers who know more than I do. Use it all. Along the way, you'll add extra tools that you've fabricated yourself until your toolbox becomes something others can borrow from you and so on.

I wrote my first book review in a little indie magazine called *Insidious Reflections*. The review was for *Only Child* by the late great Jack Ketchum. Coincidentally, Ketchum (the pen name of Dallas Mayr) was also the first author I interviewed in the winter of 2005, also for *Insidious Reflections*. These days I like to think I know what I'm doing at least slightly more than half the time, but back then? I didn't have a clue. I'll always be grateful to *Insidious Reflections* for giving me a chance and letting me cut my writing chops, even letting me publish my first short story with them, but that's a topic for another book (or not).

1

Since *Only Child*, I couldn't tell you how many reviews I've written. Seriously, I would have no idea. Back in the day, I wrote for free (or for contributor copies if I was really lucky) for small independent publications that tended not to last long before publishers were forced to close doors and get on with their lives. I still have copies of every magazine I could get a copy of back then. I'll never throw them out. I also wrote for a few websites that no longer exist; those reviews, along with various articles and interviews I did, are lost forever, as is whatever media storage I may have once saved them to. I spent several years "dabbling" with reviews, interviews, and articles for such publications as *Insidious Reflections, Dark Recesses Press, Hackers Source,* and *Fear Zone* before I started doing regular reviews and interviews for *Hell Notes* (all of which are kept archived on their site). According to those archives, my first review was of *Interloper* by Barry Hoffman at the end of 2012. A couple of years later, I would start sending over reviews to *Rue Morgue* magazine. While I've been reviewing regularly for *Rue Morgue* these past few years, it was hardly a smooth start, but more on that later. While you will also see an occasional review from me land online at *Cemetery Dance*, mostly it's my interviews you're apt to see there from me, such as my weekly interview column, What Screams May Come.

While I can't tell you how many reviews I've written since the first one, I can tell you that in 2021, I had accumulated fourteen published reviews between 2019 and 2021 because I included them in a self-published collection along with all my film reviews and interviews from that time frame. The book is called *Dark Bites: Volume 1*, and while this guide isn't meant to be an advertisement, if you're so inclined to check it out, you can always contact me, and I'll send you a free PDF. After all, if you've made it this far, we're officially friends now.

Like I said, I can only share what I know from my own experience, and that's all I plan on trying to do. I also know how frustrating it can be to go through the process of learning how to write a great review you can stand behind. Maybe you want to get paid, or maybe you just want to do the book justice so you can keep those advance reader copies (ARCs) rolling in. Whatever your end goal is for wanting to write a book review, my promise to you is I'll lay out everything I know from the years I've experienced going through the grind until I finally started getting it right enough that publications wanted to give me money to keep doing it.

Whatever you set out to do with whatever you learn from this guide, I wish nothing but the best of luck for you. Happy reading, and happy reviewing!

Rick Hipson, Summer of 2023

BOOK REVIEWS:

WHAT ARE THEY AND WHAT DO THEY DO?

IT MIGHT SEEM like an obvious question, but have you thought about what a book review is? I mean, really thought about it? What's the point of a book review? What are they supposed to do? Are they supposed to do anything?

If you're like me, when I used to think of a book review, I would often get thrown back in time to when I was in elementary school hearing the dreaded words "book report" spill out of my teacher's mouth. When I was a kid, I never liked having to write about what I thought of a book I had just finished. I just wanted to read and enjoy the bloody thing and keep my thoughts and reflections to myself. Get out of my book world, teacher! Maybe it was different for you, but I didn't enjoy writing book reports, and that's what I used to think of book reviews.

Thinking back to those days of writing book reports, it was likely just a ruse to prove we read the book, that we remembered what it was about, and were reflective enough to suggest whether it was enjoyable and worth sharing or not. There wasn't much focus (at least none I remember) about demonstrating why we thought what we thought upon finishing a book. I've no doubt a lot of folks, maybe even a few of you reading this, think writing an effective book review is as easy as writing, "The book was good. It was dark and scary and made me want to keep reading. You should read it, too." But suffice it to say, if it were that easy, you likely wouldn't be reading this guide, would you? Truth be told, a review should captivate readers enough that they want to read everything you have to say. Your review also needs to get the reader excited to read the book by helping them understand what it's about and whether they are likely to enjoy it. As with any creative endeavor, this takes work. It takes work because it takes practice. Practice takes time,

4

patience, perseverance, thick skin, and probably a moderate amount of cursing. A little insanity can go a long way, too—though it's not always necessary, it sure doesn't hurt.

Back in about 2002, I joined a little group called the Horror Library on a story writing site called *Zoetrope* (bear with me here). Times were different then. We didn't have the internet's immense network of like-minded souls who wanted to talk about the things they love and hate most that we do now. The Horror Library was a small online community of said people, and for once I felt I was truly no longer alone in my weirdverse of loving all things dark in entertainment. Here, I was free to chatter on about my favorite books and movies. Eventually, I had the urge to write about my passions and share them with the others in the group. Writing book reviews seemed like a fun way to scratch that itch.

It was through that small *Zoetrope* group that I met a ragtag group of individuals who just so happened to be insane enough to start a magazine. They invited a slew of us from the group, for some reason opting to think I was a good choice to have tag along, and called the magazine *Insidious Reflections.*

From the start, I always felt the first job a review should do is to capture the attention of readers in as clear and entertaining a way as possible. There are multiple ways to do that, which I'll delve deeper in depth about later. But if you are not intentional and succinct with every word you choose, a reader may lose focus on any valid points you're trying to convey. And, if it's not entertaining—even if it's clear—a reader won't make it through to the end of your review before getting distracted by their mental grocery list. Of course, if your review leaves them with a blah feeling about the book, then you're not exactly doing that author's book—or your time—any favours, are you? More on that later, too.

I feel like this is a good time to touch on what a book review can do. What's the point of writing one?

It's a fair question. Opinions will and should always vary, but before I give you my two cents (since I assume that's what you're all here for), here's what a few of my friends have to say about book reviews so you don't have to take only my word for it:

Joe Mynhardt, founder and CEO of Crystal Lake Publishing: "Why are reviews so important to authors and publishers (especially on Amazon)? It opens up different avenues of marketing (some places require a minimum number of reviews) and leads to better conversion rates by helping on-the-fence readers click that buy button. Plus, authors really love feedback."

Barry Hoffman, author (*Born Bad, Track of My Tears*) and publisher (Gauntlet Press Publishing): "Other than stoking the ego of an author with a good review, the main purpose of a review (to a publisher) is to stoke interest in a given book and hopefully sell some copies. Reviews are more important for newer writers who are not well-known to the general public. Getting your name out there is of tantamount importance, and that's what a review can do."

Richard Christian Matheson, author (*Zoopraxis, The Ritual of Illusion*) and screenwriter (*Battleground*): "Strong reviews are a gift. At best, they increase an author's reputation, visibility, and sales. Negative reviews, at worst, dig graves. With my work, publishers and editors usually send reviewers galleys or early copies for jacket quotes or reviews. If I know an author and sense they'll find my work interesting, I'm fine reaching out to them, especially for an introduction. Regarding a quality reviewer, tastes differ. My own top qualities are that they write with engagement that's never stuffy and remain fully immersible in what they read, not analytically hovering as if grading a test. Wit is welcome. Reviews that wound, chastise, flame-throw snark, or demean are not."

Candace Nola, author (*Bishop*), reviewer, and editor for *Uncomfortably Dark*: "Presentation, professionalism, and a striking cover all go a long way toward enticing a reader, but few things are more valuable to an author than a review. Early reviews by respected reviewers within the community give a book a leg up, so to speak, when it launches."

Reviews help readers stop and take note, read the review, look up the author, read some other reviews for their work, and hopefully purchase their new book and others. Not only do reviews help in this way but, since everything is online and at the mercy of the algorithm of most distribution platforms, reviews and ratings drive the visibility of a book higher up the algorithm, allowing it to be seen more frequently by new customers. The more reviews and/or ratings a book has, the more that platform will push it to its readers. Many readers will not stop to read more about a book if they see no ratings or no reviews. If no one else read it, why should they?

Reviews, good or bad, also allow the author to see what is working, what is not, what readers are responding to, and how they may be able to improve their craft. Sure, it's an opinion, but when many readers have the same opinion, this can go a long way toward helping an author improve their skills.

If a review manages to hit all the checkboxes—it hooks the reader's attention from the beginning, it's clear and thoughtful throughout, it gets an emotional reaction (excitement, humour, sadness), and leaves the reader wanting more from the review and from the book you're reviewing—then that review hit its target. The reader got a minute or two of entertainment, perhaps added a new book or author to their "to be read" list, or, best of all, maybe that reader went from your review all the way to the order page and bought a copy then and there. Think about it. In either of those situations, I think it's fair to say you should be happy because your review has been well-received. After all, the readers are happy because they enjoyed something you wrote, plus the author is happy because you just helped grow their fan base and perhaps even helped them buy their kid's next Happy Meal. Oh, and if you help make the author happy, there may be a residual effect that makes the book's publisher happy too because every entertaining thing on their platform will help boost their fan base and ad revenue, which goes back into keeping the whole industry alive like a not-so-proverbial circle of life.

Notice I didn't mention anything about cash when checking those checkboxes? There's a reason for that, and we'll get to it in the next chapter, I promise.

WHAT'S IN IT FOR YOU AND WHY WOULD YOU WANT TO DO THIS?

"**A**RE YOU INSANE?" "You really haven't thought this through, have you?" "HAHAHAHA!" And, "You've got your whole life ahead of you!" These are just some of the responses that come to mind whenever someone says they want to make money being a reviewer. This is often followed by a long, awkward pause before I put my hand on their shoulder and say with all the sympathy I can muster, "Run! Run very fast and very far and never look back." Usually, this is met with a blank stare and slow blinking.

Before you get the wrong impression, let me explain. I am all about writers getting paid for the words they write. Words are hard. They take time, effort, and learning the craft to make every word count. Your work deserves payment. However, we all have to start somewhere and, in the great scheme of lucrative creative ventures, book reviews are somewhere near the bottom of the heap. It's not that they aren't valued. As stated previously, a great review can have a meaningful ripple effect from reviewer to author to reader and so on. But in the business of publishing, reviews pay the least amount of bills and therefore provide the lowest payout. At least that's my experience based on my knowledge, which is by no means absolute. If you can find a publisher willing to pay a silly amount for book reviews, do me a solid and let me know, will ya?

At this point, you might be seconds away from lighting a match to this stupid guide and yelling "SCAM!" before demanding a refund. Maybe you'll even write your own (not-so-kind) review about how you were misled into thinking you could get paid to read books you love. But hold on. I'm going to do you a favour and blow out that match. Yes, later chapters will tell you how you can make some cash as a reviewer, but not yet. We've got some work to do before we get there, but rest assured, we'll get there.

Writing for free—or, if you're lucky, for contributor copies—is a great way to hone your craft as a reviewer and get your name out there so folks start to know you as a reviewer. Whether you review for a personal blog, a small indie magazine publication, or an online platform that gets ad revenue from publishers if their books get coverage, the point is to simply practice by any means necessary while building up a bit of a portfolio. (More about why that can help you later.)

This seems like a good time to remind you, if you don't know why you want to review books yet, I suggest you think hard about a reason you can stand by before you read the rest of this guidebook. Go ahead. I'll wait.

In the meantime, for those of you who are able to pull certain skills from past experiences—maybe you wrote ad copy for twenty years, for example—and found you were able to write your first review ever and get paid a fool's ransom for it while helping an author's book become a bestseller—maybe your review appeared on a billboard in Times Square, for example—then this guidebook was never meant for you. In fact, you should just stop reading now and go buy a dozen copies to give out to folks who aspire to be like you.

As for the rest of you reading, have you got a good reason for writing reviews? Good. Hold onto that and don't let go. Trust me, you're gonna need it.

To be clear, there is no bad reason for wanting to write reviews. Want free ARCs so you can read a free book before anyone else even knows it's coming out? Who doesn't? Want to chip in and help a community of writers get noticed and sell more books so they can write more stories? Also a great reason. Or maybe you read a book you enjoyed so much you have an unusual desire to share it with as many people as you can. That's a great reason, too. And if your reason is a combination of these, or something else entirely, that's cool. I have a few reasons myself why I love reviewing. Those reasons have evolved over the years as yours might. That's okay, too. This is a judgment-free zone, and we're all here to learn how to write the most effective reviews we can regardless of our reasons.

Eventually, I hope you do get paid; just know it may be a

medium to long haul until you get there, which is par for the course as I understand it.

And when you do start getting paid, how much can you expect? It depends, which I know is a crap answer, but it really does. Some online publications pay $10 USD, while I've been paid $35 CAD to see my review in a print magazine. Some pay by the word, from 1 cent to 6 cents, often with a cap on word count. $35 is the most I've been paid which is why any reviews I write will typically go to that publication. Sometimes I like to think of it as my twenty-year overnight success story because it's cool as hell to see my review in print and know I got paid a fair amount for it. There are also other ways to get paid for the work you put into a review, which I'll cover in the double-dipping section of this guide a little further on.

Oh, and let's not forget that—as a reader who likely gets a warm, gushy rush at having discovered a new favourite story and author—getting free books to review is sweet whether you do or do not get paid to write a review for it. I've had a chance to read many limited-edition books from specialty presses I couldn't have afforded to read otherwise.

I think I've exhausted this chapter. If you're new to reviewing, you're probably already thinking, "Okay, I've got a reason I want to review books, and I understand it's gonna take work to be successful at it like anything else, but how the hell do I get books to review without doing anything illegal?" Fair question, after all. Flip the page and find out, assuming you're still here after learning what a financially lucrative endeavor this isn't.

MEET THE AUTHORS!

AND GET THEIR BOOKS

G ET YOUR FLYSUIT on and find a comfy spot on my wall. It's time to take you back to when I decided the world needed this guidebook.

One time, while scrolling through my social media feeds, I noticed several authors posting about their newest releases and how they've just sent out a fresh batch of ARCs. Likewise, I also read several posts from reviewers sharing images of the shiny ARCs received in their mailboxes. (Yes, I've shared plenty of my own precious ARCs, too.) In response, several readers wished they could get in on the ARC bandwagon, and I realized that there aren't enough guidebooks for those readers who want to receive ARCs and review books. Rest assured, it's easier than you think, and your favorite authors may just thank you for it provided you approach them in a favorable manner.

First things first: Where do you find authors you enjoy reading, and how do you connect with them in a meaningful way once you've found them? Luckily, it is infinitely easier now than it used to be with almost every author having at least some kind of online presence. Keep in mind, some authors make their presence more accessible than others by having personal accounts on just about every social media outlet that exists.

The best approach to connecting with authors is often the simplest one. Whichever social media platform you use, search for the authors you have either read and enjoyed or always wanted to read. Also consider searching for authors you have generally heard a good thing or two about if you have an interest in knowing more about them and their work. Now go ahead and add/follow their group and/or personal account depending on what you find. In some cases, such as Facebook, you may need to wait until they accept your request to add them. Don't sweat it if this part takes a while; the more prolific the author, the more requests they sift through and, let's face it, we'd rather they be busy writing than stuck in social media's productivity vacuum, don't we? The point is, some may be quick to connect with while others may take a bit depending on the platform and their schedule.

Regardless of what happens once you attempt to connect with them on socials, one thing you do not—I repeat, you do NOT—want to do is to react the moment you've made the connection by jumping into their DMs and declaring how excited you are because now that you're officially friends, they can send all their ARCs to you henceforth. I'm sure none of you reading this would do exactly that, but some of you might be inclined to immediately go for the kill, so to speak. For those of you inclined to do so, I must caution you to pump the brakes just a little bit lest you come across like an annoying spammer despite your best intentions. I don't want that for you, and I'm guessing neither do you.

Speaking of caution, I would be remiss if, at this point, I didn't strongly advise anyone reading this that my suggestions to seek out authors, add them to your social platforms and message them a brief hello or admiration of their work is *not*-I repeat *not*-in any way my endorsement that you should go ahead and make out like any of these authors owe you anything. They don't owe you or I their time, their response, or anything else. It's important to realize, every author—and certainly any reader—has boundaries you do not want to push past. This goes double for women who, sadly, have most likely at some point in their writing journey been approached in a less than savory way by some creepy dude under the guise of fandom. While I am confident you and most everyone who is reading this wouldn't take the creepy approach, well, I need to do what I think is best to help cover my ass and yours. Besides, I never know who else may be reading this and therefore want to be as perfectly clear as possible. Heck, you may not even be aware that a newly approached author may be taking whatever you write as creepy, inappropriate, or generally uncool. Best practice is to always keep it professional. Keep it about their work, keep it clean and, while you might feel complimenting them on their looks, using sexual innuendos or blatant sarcasm is charming, humorous, or otherwise endearing, it simply is not. The last thing you want is to be labeled as an inappropriate creeper who just made yet another woman or person of minority feel uncomfortable in any way, intended or otherwise. The writing community we all love is a big one, but a tight knit one and writers, publishers, and readers alike do talk to each other. The golden rule applies, and I hope if you get approached by fellow readers and/or writers, that they abide by the above common decency for your sake as well as that of our community. Let's keep it classy for everyone, folks.

Alright, so what the heck do you do once you've connected then? Try saying hi. Say what? Say hi. Tell them you're happy to be connected online. That you've heard good things about their work and are looking forward to getting to know them and their work better. If you've not read an author who is now connected with you on your social platform of choice, then by all means ask the author where they recommend you start with their work, maybe after suggesting the type of stories you usually enjoy.

Alternatively, you can also do what I do and simply add authors to your social media feeds and comment accordingly on occasional posts you enjoy from them. I guarantee you they will eventually make announcements of upcoming work, which is a perfectly reasonable time to send a brief, kind message asking if they would like to include you in their list of reviewers to help promote their new book. I wouldn't ask for one just yet. Let the author take the lead. They may ask where you would publish the review and, based on where it might be going (such as a popular site or a reputable print magazine), they may even offer to give you a free copy. Whatever they recommend, go ahead and grab it if and when you can. The idea here, as you've no doubt gathered, is to approach them like you would anyone with whom you'd like to connect, not as someone you want something from.

Of course, this never guarantees you'll be sent an ARC. Don't take it personally and be sure to thank them all the same. I don't think it would hurt you to ask their reason in the hopes you might better position yourself to be a reviewer for them in the future, though I tend to simply move on and continue to focus on the reviews of books I do get access to. Keep in mind that some publishers have to be very picky about where ARCs go. They may only have so many physical copies available (due to many factors, increased costs associated with publishing chief among them) and may reserve them for publications they feel will cast the most eyeballs on a review.

For example, back when I was reviewing for *Hell Notes* (a great place to start although they don't pay), I once asked a pretty prolific author whom I've heard nothing but praise about if I could review their upcoming book. It sounded intriguing as hell, and I was sure I would enjoy it and review it favorably. The author either wasn't familiar with *Hell Notes* or felt the book would be better off getting reviewed by a larger, more influential publication, and so he denied me an ARC. I was bummed for about 15 minutes, but I understood. Physical ARCs can be expensive, especially when mailing to Canada (via moose and buggy, it would seem), and publishers have to be picky about where their limited ARCs get sent to. Thanks to the advent of digital technology, PDF files are much more likely to be sent your way as an ARC, although some publishers still do send the physical stuff, which I for one really friggin' appreciate, considering the added cost.

This isn't to say that your favorite author who just announced an upcoming release won't send you an ARC for you to review. That could happen depending on who your favorite author is and what criteria they have for sending out a review copy. Every author and book release is different, and all you can do is ask.

Even if more popular authors decline your offer to review, the internet has made it easier for rising independent authors to break through and get their work out there. While there is a lot more work to sift through—and not all great or good—there are plenty of outstanding stories making their way to the surface. And considering how pricey and time-consuming a sound marketing strategy can be, most indie authors (as well as long-standing small press authors) will generally be happy to provide a review copy as long as the review appears somewhere potential readers can see it.

If you have a hard time securing ARCs from authors or publishers directly, eBooks are a great way to read on a budget if you have the option and can read digitally. You can often take advantage of 99-cent deals or limited-time freebies.

Then, once you've read the book, give it an honest review to the best of your abilities and post it where you have access to post reviews whether it's on a website, print publication, personal blog, or on Amazon where you can help the algorithm push the book and potentially get some extra sales for the author. All you have is a WordPress blog? Great! You can post your review there and link to it easy-peazy. What's that? You don't have a blog, want nothing to do with them, and just want to read no-cost stories in exchange for helping an author and their work? Cool! You can still leave a review on Amazon, which helps support the algorithm and gets the book shown to more readers. It's also a great excuse for the author to post another link for your review and hype their book further (that way they get more sales and can therefore write more books).

The point is, as long as you are willing to read the book, consider how you felt about the book, and provide an honest, well-crafted review of the book, then you're still honing your review chops, building a portfolio, and still supporting your community of authors. I guarantee, especially if the author isn't expecting it, they will be quite grateful for the unsolicited support. That's how you build a network of authors willing to work with you without coming across as a spammer, stalker, or just another random person trying to get something from them.

Wherever you decide to place your review, send the link to the author and thank them for the recommendation. When they respond, let them know that if ever they wish to have you review any of their other books (or ones that may be coming out in the future), to please let you know as you would be happy to do so. And bam! You now have an author who will likely appreciate your support, not feel pressured by you, and may actually keep you in mind when their next book comes out.

That's ultimately how you build your opportunities as a reviewer and as a writer in general. One connection, one step, one project at a time. Eventually, your opportunities will expand, and you'll be ready to aim your efforts at the bigger publishers with some quality samples to showcase your chops. And, when you get your chance to shine, your hard work will pay off as you begin to send them well-written reviews on the regular. Such reviews will open the doors to those authors and publishers who prefer to send ARCs to reviewers who will publish on the biggest, most influential platforms and attract the most potential buyers for their books. Before you know it, you'll have a respectable stable of authors and publishers with whom you can stay connected in case they need a reviewer like you.

But what if you have trouble finding authors online or wish to expand from the ones you already know about? Don't worry, I've got you covered there, too.

Facebook specifically, no matter your personal thoughts about the platform, is an endless haven of fan pages and groups. It's as simple as plugging your favorite genre, sub-genre, or author into the search field. You're bound to be met with tons of options for joining and interacting with like-minded people. Although this guidebook and my advice within it can pertain to any and all genres, I'm a horror guy at heart, so that's where my specialty as far as experience and knowledge rests. From my experience, hands down the best book group I have been a part of is called Books of Horror. With over 40,000 current members, it's filled to the brim with passionate readers as well as a plethora of authors and publishers from all walks of style and life. The group is surprisingly well-kept and mostly free of drama. This is thanks to a dedicated team of moderators whose number one goal is to make it the most accessible and fan-friendly group on Facebook, which I think they are succeeding at.

Prolific author Brian Keene also has a great forum he's created where several authors and publishers co-mingle. It's a cross between the newsgroups of old (anyone remember Shocklines?) and a friendly group you might find on Facebook without having to actually be on Facebook. You can get there by plugging https://thekeenedom.freeforums.net/ into your browser and interacting there.

Goodreads is also a great option for joining various groups and seeking out what others are reading. Also, it is a great platform where readers discover books they want to read. Goodreads reviews really help authors out. Plus, it's an easy place to post reviews and an accessible method for honing your reviewing chops while building your reputation.

I would also suggest Reddit as another great resource though, I admit, I don't spend nearly as much time exploring that neck of the cyber woods as I probably should. Likewise, there are plenty of social media platforms where writers can connect, such as BlueSky (if you can nail down a passkey or whatever they're calling it to get in), Substack, and others like X (formerly known as Twitter) and Threads.

Just make sure you don't join all these extra platforms for the sake of joining. Otherwise, you may get so overwhelmed and overburdened that you end up souring the personal reward factor of being a part of various writing communities. Also, if you want to read and review outside the horror genre, go ahead and join groups and forums that revolve around whichever genre or subgenre you have an interest in engaging in and supporting. The possibilities are truly endless.

If you prefer to stay off social media or simply don't feel the need to depend on it (who could blame you?), Netgalley is also a fantastic way to find authors, publishers, and their ARCs. It offers a cornucopia of book titles of all genres and makes it easy to search for the books you're most interested in reading. Found a great book? Not only are their purchase links available, but you can also request an ARC with the click of a button. Your ARC request might still get rejected for any number of reasons, but getting rejected has never been more convenient, and there really is plenty of selections to try again with. Besides, if you don't ask, the answer will always be the same.

Another benefit of Netgalley is if you plan to post your review in written or video form on social platforms, each book title also provides recommended hashtags to use in the description.

If you're an author and reading this guidebook, Netgalley is a two-way street and has much to benefit you by giving a direct link to you and your reviewers and letting you pick which reviewers you want covering your work. Likewise, Bookfunnel is another great resource for providing promotional platforms and helping to streamline the link between you and readers. Having multiple outlets and formats of your work being made available in one simple destination is a major plus, and no, they didn't pay me to say that.

Aside from the above, never be afraid to approach a publisher directly to ask for a title of theirs to review, or if they have any upcoming publications they may like to have you cover for them. If you can't find them on the socials, you can often seek out a contact on their website. Even if their site only offers a generic contact form, my experience suggests most publishers will get back to you most of the time.

Okay, we've got the ARC. Now how the heck do we write a review that resonates with readers that any publication would be happy to publish and give us money for?

If you made it this far, then it's time to get to the nuts and bolts of it and show you how I learned to do it so you can do it, too.

HOW IT'S DONE ACCORDING TO ME

FROM WHAT I'VE FOUND, nobody wants to pay you to practice writing, which is to say you have to start somewhere. My best advice? Start by reading reviews. Seriously, why take the time to mess around trying to get it right, when you can read the culmination of somebody else's sweat, blood, and cursing? Naturally, book reviews that resonate are personal things, but I suggest you cut out or bookmark any review that entertained you and made you keen to read the book. Chances are these are the sort of reviews you are likely to enjoy writing yourself. Consider what made you feel the way you feel. Consider the style of the review, the words chosen, the number of words used. How did they describe the way the book made them feel? On the flip side, take note of reviews that totally didn't work for you, and consider why. Was the review boring? Did it ramble incoherently without making any clear points? Did it describe a book that simply isn't for you? Lessons from a poorly written review can be just as beneficial as you learn to craft a great review—maybe even more so because they stick out like a sore thumb. It's up to you to realize why and practice your reviews accordingly. Heck, I've been doing this long enough for it to be considered a life sentence (minus time for good behavior, of course), and I still enjoy reading weak reviews to keep myself up to speed with what doesn't work and why. In fact, I read as many reviews as possible to see what works well—and what doesn't—no matter the style the reviewer went with.

That said, the last thing I want for you is to write weak reviews after all we've been through in this guide. It's time we get to work on how to make sure you write the best reviews you're capable of and, with some luck and determined work, how to get paid doing it.

Consider this the nuts-and-bolts section of this guidebook.

A REVIEWER'S GUIDE TO WRITING BOOK REVIEWS

Maybe some of you have already screamed at me to "Don't Bore Us, Get to the Chorus" and wondered what the hell all this prattling on is about. If you're only here to learn how to craft a solid book review and maybe make a few bucks doing it, then this next bit is exactly what you've been waiting for!

Before we continue, let me repeat that the way I write my reviews and the suggestions I give are just that: my suggestions. I'm confident in my ability to write a good (and sometimes even a great) review after practicing for the last 20 years and now publishing in some of the biggest publications in our industry, but that doesn't mean I know everything or that my way and advice is the best there is. I encourage you all to take everything I suggest as just another tool to add to your collection for you to use when needed. Please do seek out other reviewers' advice. Everyone has their own style and methods for what works best for them. Which is why my first bit of advice is always that: If you want to learn how to write, then you must learn to be a voracious reader. There's a reason you're probably sick of hearing that advice across the board. It works.

Grab your favourite magazine and read the review section (if there is one). Go online to those sites you bookmarked before and read as many reviews as you can. Go on Amazon or Goodreads and search for reviews of books you've read or might like to read. Study them. Ingest them. Rip the pages out and chew on them for a while (okay, maybe not that last part, but you get the idea, right?). Get a feel for which reviews caught your attention early on and kept it. Did the review intrigue you? Entertain you? Make you want to read a book, or make you know a certain book is likely not for you? Was it boring? Confusing? Did you stop reading before it was done? Why? Think long and hard about why the review made you feel the way it did. Was it the style of the review, or something else altogether? Or maybe it was a combination of things. Make a note, either a mental note or a physical one. Whatever works for you. Try keeping a collection of your favourite reviews and those you felt just plain suck. Use them as examples of what to do and what not to do when you write your reviews.

Before you even set out to write a review, you must first have a solid handle on the lines you will be coloring in, so to speak. Mainly, you need to know if you have a word count to consider. If you're writing for your blog, the word count is entirely up to you.

Write a thousand words if you wish, a hundred thousand, though you probably want to make sure it doesn't exceed the attention or the life span of whoever is likely to read it. Personally, I don't think any book review should exceed 500 words, and even that length starts to border on essay.

Call me biased (you'd probably be right) but, since I've been writing reviews for *Rue Morgue Magazine*, I think a great review can and should be told in as close to about 300 words as possible. That's *Rue's* word count limit due to space and the preference they have (although their Dante's Picks reviews are allotted 350 words). While I admit that sometimes I wish I had more space, I've never felt I was short-changing a reader by maxing my reviews at about the 300-word limit.

It always amazes me how my first drafts differ from my final drafts, even if by word count alone. I often start messy and put as much down about the book and then trim from there, cutting out all the unimportant fillers and tightening up to the point where every word counts and earns its keep. I've often started out with a bloated 500 words, sometimes much more, only to have to bring it down to 300. It's not easy, especially when you write what you feel is your best line ever but then have to cut it out because it just doesn't add any value to the overall review. Stephen King calls it killing your darlings. I don't think of it so much as killing my darlings but more like beating them back with a stick and sending them off to go play somewhere else. And don't worry, I'll be giving you some examples of this process a little later, I promise. I've got your back.

I also find it amazing how much of what you think should go into a review really isn't necessary. A great exercise is to go ahead and write a review of anything, maybe the last book you read or of something else, anything. Don't make it too long, but go ahead and fire off a few hundred words in the form of a review. Don't worry about making it good or even great, just get it down.

Go ahead and do that now, and I'll be here when you're done.

Got your review? Good. Now take that review and condense it into a 70-word review. No seriously, give it a try. Not easy, is it? But with practice, you'll be able to pull it off and realize how well you can take a handful of words and condense them to their barest bones in order to get the same message across to the reader, except, instead of meandering like a lion slowly stalking its prey in the wilds of the jungle, your message hits them fast and hard like an arrow to the brain.

Back when *Rue Morgue* had their Grim Reader section, they would publish reviews of about 60–70 words. I owe a ton of gratitude to this section because it was my training ground for learning the importance of taking 10 words and boiling them down to only one or two words. Those little Grim reviews were an excellent exercise in minimalism. Give them a try. They'll sharpen your work and teach you how to zero in on what's most vital to convey in a review. Take a chance and try writing a mini-review. Don't worry; you can always expand if needed after you've got the barest of bones to work with so long as whatever you add gives more value to the review.

Here's a 60-word review I did for the Grim Reader back in the day before I convinced the editors I was ready to contribute more elaborate reviews. This one was for *Keepers of The Dead*, by Bob Freeman:

Keepers of the Dead will have you clawing the pages past midnight as vamps and beasties bid war upon the existence of mankind. Bob's imagination expertly fuses with occult wisdom to satiate anyone's craving for a little blood, adventure, and a finale that'll tear breath from mortal lungs. Welcome to a world of dark fantastic. The wolves of Cairnwood await.

Doesn't tell you a lot about the book, does it? But I think it tells you enough to know if you might want to read this book. It has an opening hook to catch your attention, a brief summary of what kind of story you can expect, and leaves with a closing call to action that is intended to leave you wanting to read more of the review and the book.

As I explained before, some of my reviews started at 300 words or more, and then I had to whittle it down to its barest necessity. Here's an example of me doing exactly that with a novel called *Ulrik* by Stephen E. Wedel.

First, here's the full-length review of 248 words:

School teacher and contributing editor for *Horror World*, Steve Wedel re-invents the werewolf legacy with *Ulrik*, book four of the Werewolf Saga. While knowledge of the saga's predecessors might accentuate this feast, it won't rob you of enjoying this tale as a singular, adrenaline-packed treat. Wedel takes surgical care to weave in just enough backstory without being intrusive or long in the tooth.

When Shara Wellington's cure for lycanthropy has worn out its effect on her eight-year-old son, life gets complicated. But when the rebellious pup runs away in wolf form and is hunted down and snatched up by the queen of all bitches, Kiona Brokentooth, things get even hairier.

Thinking her husband killed, Shara puts faith in the only creature she can—a rogue werewolf named Thomas who saves her shape-shifting skin from a vicious group attack on her home. Not knowing who to count on, but knowing there are many who want her dead, Shara must choose between turning her back on rescuing her son— and quite likely having to kill her mentor, Ulrik, in the process—or calling out to the sleeping wolf within her and assuming her prophetic role as Mother of the Pack.

With an imminent war bringing the pack to gather, it's only a matter of time before the snare snaps shut and traps Shara in an unbreakable fate of pain and suffering. With Steve's pure and easy form, it's clear that there shall be no culls among us here.

Now, here's the condensed 70-word version:

When Shara's son is kidnapped to oblige her mentor's personal agenda, the fur begins to fly in this adrenaline-fuelled reinvention of the lycanthropic world. Shara must now give in to her inner bitch and accept her prophetic role as

Mother of the Pack, or they're all doomed. Written in a style that's simple, raw, fierce, and merciless, Ulrik will seduce readers into leaving the path and running with the wolves.

Once again, all the aspects are there in condensed detail within the mini-review, proving that despite what we may feel, it is possible to say a lot with very little. Which version is better? That's up to the reader to decide, and each of you as well. Personally, I like them both, but obviously the first gave me extra wiggle room to divulge a few more details about what the book is about; I like to think it also gives the reader a bit more ammo for choosing to buy the book or not. The main point I'm trying to make is that learning to tell compelling reviews in as little space as possible is bound to benefit you the way it has benefited me. The easier a review is to digest, the more it will resonate with a reader and the easier it will be for them to decide if this is a book for them.

That said, if you have a chance to use unique metaphors or a different style of prose in order to convey the feel of a book, by all means go for it, as long as it suits the book you're reviewing.

For example, here's a review I wrote for *Rue Morgue* for a book that tested how many times you could roll your eyes at a collection of Dad-worthy monster jokes and puns. Considering the content of the book, the last thing I wanted to do was take a serious approach to my review. Also, this is a decent example of reviewing a book that, while not among my top reads for that year, had enough enjoyable parts that I could focus on for a mostly positive review.

This review was for *Ha-Ha Horror Collector's Edition* from Monster Matt Patterson.

The man of a thousand bad monster jokes is back with his latest installment of stunners and shunners. Running the full gamut of horror icons from Dracula to Creature from the Black Lagoon to Street Trash to Slime City and everything in between, no monster is left untormented or unmashed by Patterson's zany antics. All manner of horror fare is fed through the demented joke-grinding device lurking in the depths of Matt's

strange subconscious and spit out on the pages. You'll groan, you'll chortle, you'll cry. Heck, you'll probably end up blowing milk out your nose and hugging your knees pondering what life choices that led you here, and that's just the first chapter. Will you make it to the end before ripping out your funny bone and beating yourself into oblivion with it? Consider yourself triple dog dared.

Each chapter is kept brief and lean, a small but courteous mercy from the author. As an allegory to Patterson's favorite monster movies, each chapter is introduced with a short history about whichever film is about to be mocked. A standout for me is the few chapters showcasing Patterson's artwork, which I found to be an enjoyable throwback to the gleefully macabre monsters I loved as a kid, complete, of course, with groan-worthy captions. As if knowing readers will inevitably seek out sharp objects by the book's conclusion, the collection also includes a section of dismembered monster parts to cut out and mix and match to your weird heart's content should you be so inclined.

As a special bonus, here's one not in the collection: What do you get when you cross this book with a sucker who'll try anything to remedy a nagging horror/comedy craving? Mental mutilation by a thousand puns. You're welcome.

As you can see, while I took the liberty to try and match the wacky style of the book and certainly had fun using descriptions and a style I don't normally use, I kept it all about the book. I didn't stray into the woods chasing zebras by way of my own flowery prose for the sake of showcasing my chops above the author whose work I'm reviewing. I think I managed that with this review and hopefully, you can spot that, too.

Speaking of getting lost in the forest, I don't know about you, but my enjoyment of a book doesn't always equal a detailed recollection of all the things I enjoyed about the book. If the book happened to have a fairly complicated storyline with multiple layers, chances are high that relaying what made it work so well will be a challenge. Same for anthologies or short story collections. Even more so if you happen to have ADHD, whether it's an official diagnosis or an obvious likelihood. There have also been times when, for various reasons, I was unable to get to writing a review until weeks after reading the book. As much as I like to think nobody noticed while reading those reviews, there's no denying I wouldn't have had to work quite so hard to hit my deadline if I had written the review immediately after I read the book. Or if I took notes. But let's talk about taking notes later. For now, let's get you armed you with some razor-sharp hooks you can't do without, and no, I'm not talking about fishing. Or am I?

HOOK 'EM FAST, HOOK 'EM HARD

EVER START A book or movie and within a few minutes, you're thinking to yourself, *Yes! This is exactly what I'm in the mood for and I can't wait to keep going*. That's a great feeling, isn't it? It's our job to elicit that feeling from readers as much as we can in our reviews. You may only be asking a reader to invest a couple of minutes of their lives into reading your review of a few hundred words, but every second counts, and if you don't give them a reason to read past the first sentence or two, they won't. No doubt, plenty of readers likely skim over the review section in their latest issue of whatever publication they have picked up. Most want to get in, decide if the book in question is for them, and get out. This means our job as reviewers is to help them decide that the review, which we put our time and energy into, is worth their time to the end.

But how do we do it? Your own unique style, even if you don't think you have one, has a lot to do with writing a great hook. I could give examples throughout the history of literature, but if you've ever read a book with a great hook, you know the ones that worked for you. Since that may have just come across as crappy do-it-yourself advice, let me do the best I can to explain what elements I think make an effective hook.

Regardless of what we're writing, a hook should never meander. It should never be overly descriptive or need a build-up. It should be *in medias res*, in the action. It should be clear and concise, leaving nothing up for interpretation. A great hook should hit readers straight between the eyes with the kind of clear impact that leaves them knowing exactly where they are and where they're headed.

When it comes to review hooks, it's worth considering the overall impact of the book, the general way it made you feel, and what the core of the story is all about when you boil it down to its

26

rawest ingredients. It should set the stage for what we are about to receive, expanding as the review continues, but always the first step in building enough intrigue is ensuring that readers will have no choice but to finish reading the review whether they're aware they've been intentionally hooked or not.

I'm sure you can likely come up with several examples yourselves of great hooks from reviews you've read or out of the many books you've enjoyed over your life as a reader. For the sake of this guide, here are some examples of hooks from reviews I've written that I believe landed well and helped showcase my point. I don't think it matters what the book I reviewed is, but I do think it's important to explain why I think they worked.

EXAMPLE 1
It's scary enough knowing a monster is living within the tranquility of your beloved small town, but it's even worse knowing the monster may well be one of your own, someone you know, possibly someone you grew up with.

I really like this hook because not only does it capture the essence of what the book is all about, but it makes readers ask, "Who do I know that might be a monster? Damn, I better read this to find out." It creates a sense of curiosity. If I challenged you to consider one of your friends might be a monster, wouldn't you want to keep reading if only to see what the heck I might be talking about?

EXAMPLE 2
Capturing the heart of John Urbancik's podcasts across 2017 and 2018, *InkStained* proves essential reading for any writer looking to hone their craft.

What makes this hook work are two things. Again, it creates a sense of curiosity. If you're a writer wanting to hone your craft, then you know you're in the right place. Second, if you're familiar with the author, then you know right off the bat this book could be for you.

EXAMPLE 3
Rebecca Rowland once told me there are three types of cannibals: the necessity to survive at all costs type, the extreme fetish for pleasure type, and those in the middle

who started as the first type, then discovered they kinda liked it.

Again, curiosity is key. Why the hell would anyone like being a cannibal, even if only kinda? Plus, anyone who enjoys reading about cannibals and the kind of extreme horror that comes from them will know up front they may have found something that's been written just for them.

EXAMPLE 4

Flawlessly designed to rip the blinders off anyone trying to ignore the everyday terrors of hateful oppression, LaRocca proves himself a provocative force of brutal nature.

This hook tells the reader without a doubt what this book has set out to do. If readers trust my review, then they'll trust that the book pulled it off flawlessly, and who doesn't want that? And apparently the terrors within the book are ones they can relate to on an everyday basis. But they'll have to read on if they want to know what makes the author so provocative.

EXAMPLE 5

The Writing Life **packs a bevy of wisdom from the writer next door, the guy who always says hello or talks about the weather from over the fence while plotting murder under the most hilarious of circumstances.**

I like this one because it summarizes what the book is about—sharing writerly wisdom—in a very short space. Plus, I think it offers plenty of intrigue by contrasting an image of a friendly next-door neighbor with that of a madman who wants to kill . . . somebody, but how could that possibly be hilarious? Guess the reader will have to keep reading the review to find out. (See what I did there?)

You get the point. An effective hook should draw out curiosity, intrigue the reader, and let them know what they're in for when they read your review, so they have no choice but to read the next sentence, and the next, and so on.

As far as when to craft the hook, I generally do this when I sit down to write the first draft of my reviews. This might seem obvious, and I know there are other ways to do it too. Hell, I've

A REVIEWER'S GUIDE TO WRITING BOOK REVIEWS

written down what the plot was about before I even thought about how I would start the review. There may have been an occasion or two when I wrote the closing hook and then worked backward. Luckily, nobody has to know your process, however weird it might be as long as the whole of the thing works when completed. Mind you, I always found it more difficult to write the way I just described, and it was usually indicative of not knowing where to begin. Generally, though, I tend to start with a great hook, and that sets the tone for my review, and then everything else flows from there.

Exactly how I follow my hook varies book by book, for the most part. If the main effect the book had on me was to make me feel a certain way or perhaps make me consider the world in a much different light, then I might start out by conveying that first. If the book presented a story that was fascinating to me in some unique way, maybe the way it was constructed kept me guessing or its style made the most mundane event come across as captivating, then I might start there. Other times, I simply summarize the plot and then move on with my takeaways along with examples of what worked for me and, if necessary, what didn't. I'll give you a few examples in a bit to showcase a few of my different approaches and why but, for now, let me go over how to leave your readers wanting more at the end of a review.

ALWAYS LEAVE 'EM WANTING MORE

BELIEVE IT OR NOT, conclusions need hooks too. And while a concluding hook may not be quite as vital as an opening hook, it's a close second. After all, how many times have we read something enjoyable, loving every minute of it, and anticipating an end to really nail our experience only to reach a conclusion that feels every bit like the leaky tire that just ran over a nail? A crap ending can leave a reader let down, wishing the lackluster payoff made our investment worth the trip. Even though a review is far less of a time investment than a full-length novel, don't we owe it to our readers to leave them with a sense of satisfaction? Not doing so sells them and our review short (not to mention the author who entrusted you to craft a solid review for their book).

While concluding a review with some snappy cliché like "highly recommend it" or "you're going to love this book" or something equally generic might seem like a great call to action, it isn't. Sure, it's not wrong to think of your review as an entertaining sales pitch, because a great review should help a reader desire to buy the book. However, blanket statements are lazy, unoriginal, and easily forgettable. You recommend it highly? I'm going to love this book? Great! Tell me why. Better yet, use your review to express why this book is—or isn't—great for me. And, if your review is a warning for readers to avoid a book, that's fine, but then I'd have to wonder why you bothered to waste your time reading a book you hated and writing a review about it instead of finding one you enjoy more.

Alright, so if that's the gist of what a "bad" concluding hook is, then what makes a "good" one? Obviously, how good or how bad one is is subjective to the reader, which is why I framed the words with quotations, but I do believe there is a not-so-fine line between an effective one and a forgettable one that has no use other than fattening up the word count for the sake of. When done right, it will summarize the effect of the book you just told us about. It will make us feel the way you felt when you read it. It will leave a lingering taste making us want to know more, want to read more, want to buy and read the book to find out for ourselves. It's a call to action without being a blatant call to action, if that makes sense. A good final hook, much like a good opening hook, should provide a sense of curiosity that can only be satisfied by a reader putting the book in their hands and experiencing it for themselves.

Based on my points above, here are a few samples to show you what I mean from reviews I feel did a good job executing an effective concluding hook.

Example 1

Chasing The Boogeyman is a metafictional masterpiece that all but demands to be revisited and examined long after the final pages have been turned and put to rest.

I think this works because it summarizes what type of book the review references, thus letting the reader know if they're the type who is most likely to enjoy it. It also gives the idea that this book will resonate and be remembered long after they've finished the book, and who doesn't like a book that can do that?

Example 2

Feral monster mayhem with a twist of humanity at its best.

An effective finishing hook doesn't have to be long in the tooth. This one emphasizes that, if the reader enjoys monster stories that employ a sense of humanity, then they should expect to enjoy this one, too.

Example 3

While the Darkness may well feast on your conscience long after the final page is read, do yourself a favor and devour this one while there's still a little light left.

Alright, I admit it: I tried to be sneaky and break my own general rule about not blatantly telling a reader I recommend a book. I think I still nailed an effective hook all the same because my recommendation came across as something they should do before it's too late. I tried to convey that being hopeful for the world was important to get the most out of this book and that this book would validate that despite some of the uglier, darker aspects of the world they live in. At least that was my intent. What do you think? Whether you agree or not, I believe your consideration will help you better understand why it did or didn't work for you, leaving you to improve your own craft accordingly.

Example 4
Expect to leave the table with your mind twisted, your heart ablaze and your appetite satiated—for now—from the rich stew of talent cooking between these pages.

What works in this example is I give the reader an exact expectation of how I believe they're likely to feel after reading this anthology. And, if my review up to that point was crafted to the best of my ability, chances are the reader will have no reason to expect any different, and they're left feeling this ought to be a good book to get.

Example 5
What will *InkStained* do for you? Your mileage may vary, but you don't want to miss finding out.

I realize this example flirts dangerously close to a blatant recommendation, but since the book in review is a writing advice book, I wanted to give the reader a sense that if they didn't read this book, THIS book, then they would be truly missing out on getting the quality advice they need. I like to think this hook also came across as a cheeky challenge to the reader. Did they come away thinking, "Why, I'll show you what it can do"? I like to think a few may have.

I could go on, but pretty sure I just saw one of you take a chunk out of that #2 pencil you like to keep around for fidgeting purposes. It's okay. I get it. Time to move on.

But what a minute! I went over writing an opening hook, I went over writing a concluding hook, but what about all that stuff in between? You know, the actual review part of the review?

How could I forget? Honest, I didn't. The fact is there's nothing worse than feeling lost when you set out to share what made you fall in love with the last book you read. After all, how are you going to lead a reader to feel the same sense of passion you came away with if you can't draw out even a simple map of your experience?

A REVIEWER'S GUIDE TO WRITING BOOK REVIEWS

The good news as I see it is this: If you know where you are (opening hook) and you know where you're headed (closing hook), then you'll never be lost. You just have to look around and decide where to go after that opening and how to navigate arriving at the conclusion. If it sounds simple, that's because it is. It can also be the most painstakingly frustrating place to be in.

Not to worry though, because I'm here to help you set your compass so you'll always be confident about how to get from point "A" to point "B" mostly unscathed even if the direction seems far from clear at the time you need it to be.

REVIEWING 101

R EADY OR NOT, it's time to piece together everything we've gone over thus far. Hopefully, some of my ideas will make more sense as we take everything into consideration and drive it home for one common purpose: writing a professional review and getting paid for it.

In this section, I'll use some of my previously published reviews as examples of the stuff I'll be covering. I'll also use some of my early drafts to demonstrate how I personally get from point "A" (reading the book) to point "B" the final, publishable draft. Maybe point "B" should be changed to point "E" or point "H" because the road between the first and final draft isn't always short and clear—at least not for me. I think it's also important for me to show examples of first drafts to final drafts so, if for no other reason, you can see that if I can publish something that, at first, looks like it might have been squeezed out of a tube found on the side of a street and fed to a blender, then your first drafts can also be made into something publishers want to trade you cash for, if that's your goal.

I've broken down my general process in order of what I tend to do first. I say "general" because while my process is usually the same, sometimes I skip a few steps. Occasionally, I'll go from reading the last page in a book to sitting down and writing out a complete draft that only takes a quick polish or two before I send it off for publication. However, since those occurrences are rather rare, I'll focus on how most of my reviews go, which I feel will also offer the most for you to learn from.

To put it in a nutshell, a rough process for me entails making notes as I read, converting the notes into complete sentences (if required), ordering my notes so they make sense to me and so that they occur in a logical sequence for the reader, and then fleshing out my notes so that I expand on my thoughts and ideas with examples.

From there, I'll trim the fat and get rid of anything that distracts from the main points I'm trying to make. I'll also trim anything that bogs the review down (a.k.a. boring/awkward /rambling) and make sure each sentence is clear, concise, and not bloated.

Then, with what I consider a working draft, I'll add any details I think will best hammer home whatever points I'm trying to make and aspects of my thoughts about the book I may have neglected to include in my last draft. Finally, I will give a last polish focusing on meeting my word count (usually about 300 words) and ensuring my review is as tight as can be while putting across the thoughts I feel will best represent the work I am reviewing.

Let's break it down!

TAKE NOTE(S)

FIRST, IF YOU have a "type A" personality or are well-organized, whether by instinct or successful practice, then go ahead and skip this next section. You'll only laugh or say "duh" out loud a lot. For people like me who dream of being naturally organized the way a chicken might dream of flying, then this section might be the best thing you'll read in the next half hour.

Writing notes while you read can be an excellent way to keep your instant reactions and immediate takeaways from a story. I'll be the first to admit I don't do this as much as I should, but the times I have I can assure you it led to a quicker process from first draft to final draft on top of contributing to a much more effective review overall. Sometimes I get so caught up in a great book I don't want to interrupt the experience in order to write stuff down, so I'll often jot down some notes as soon as I can to summarize what I last read. The nice thing is most of us have cell phones and can easily use the notes function to throw down a few bullet points after a chapter or an especially powerful scene and get back to the action, which goes toward creating a more concise, honest, and accurate snapshot of whatever experience a certain book gave you. And remember: If you can convey that to a reader, it's the next best thing to telepathy and the best way to ensure readers who might enjoy the book buy and enjoy it as well.

Sure, writing notes as you read isn't necessary; some of you might even find writing them as you go to be too annoying or distracting to be bothered—and that's perfectly fine—but I personally recommend them. I envy the reader who can recite complete passages and describe the finer details of an intricate, complex plot long after a book has been put down, but I for one am not that reader. There have been times when, for one reason or another, I had to write a review weeks after reading a book, and while I always pulled it off well enough, I've always found it more enjoyable, less time-consuming, and far less exhausting to write from notes, even if I may not sit down straight away to write the review. Plus, I also feel that, by recording my immediate thoughts, reactions, and takeaways as I'm reading, I'm able to capture the moment and convey it in as honest a way as possible to potential readers. It's all about helping readers experience the book as you experienced it while you were experiencing it. I think this approach shows in your review even if it isn't conscious.

How you take notes is completely up to you. Bullet points? Fragmented sentences? Fully thought-out sentences? Your call entirely. My immediate thoughts as I read usually form as full sentences, so that's how I write them. Sometimes single words will pop into my head, so I write those down the way they come to me. Often, it's a mixture of both. You get to choose which of your notes go into your review and which ones stay put, never to see the light of publication. Maybe you don't even use your notes in your review but instead use them to inspire something else entirely. As long as it works for you to get the end result you're after, that's all that matters. Your notes don't need to resemble your final draft; they just have to help you get there.

Here's an example of some notes I jotted down as I read Aaron Dries's short story collection *Cut To Care: A Collection Of Little Hurts* with all the warts and errors as I wrote them:

Dries illustrates the markings of caring, of overextending ourselves for the sake of another, with scars that haunt us like ghosts we can never be rid of because given enough time and enough caring these scars—these ghosts—become who we are.

If Jack Ketchum with his emotionally charged one-two gut punches, Stephen King with his relatable small-town horror and Clive Barker with his beautifully morbid sexuality got together for the world's most terrifying orgy and forgot to use protection, then Aaron Dries would no doubt be the bastard child which crawled from the collective womb of their tryst.

The style of prose and its language isn't so

beautifully effective and seductively poetic its engagement that its damn near impossible to draw a line between the point of unassuming and the point of realization that you're not getting out of this book alive or, at the very least, without bearing a few lingering scars of your own. But remember, it's only because of how Dries cares that he cuts to mark you with stories with every intention of getting to you core where (apparently, I was interrupted writing this note)

A collective barrage of scars and bruises meant to batter you beneath the weight of its pain until you're forced to care, if only for the sake of your own sanity as it's worn down to its base level.

At first, these stories might stand out as a warning against caring. It certainly demands its reader to ask the question, is caring worth it? If for you, the answer is yes, then this book should be your stark reminder that you best make it worth it. Make it count because to care may be to cut against the fabric of yourself and burrow within a place beneath your surface to haunt your best intentions.

As you can see, these notes kind of ramble on and are in no way concise. It also doesn't tell you much about what any of the stories are really about. Instead, it shows what I was thinking as I read the book and represents my meandering brain. A lot of this didn't make it into the final draft for good reason. But these notes gave me a point of reference and a springboard on which to jump off when I sat down to write a working draft.

Believe it or not, I used these messy notes to end up with the draft below. See if you can figure out why I made some of the editorial changes I made. Hopefully, you see I cleaned things up and expanded on my thoughts to convey them in a way that might actually lead a reader to want to read this book.

Through a collection of outstanding nightmares (with an intro from Mick Garris), we can't help but inherit the markings of intense caring after being

awarded with an assortment of scars that haunt like ghosts. Given enough time, these scars—these ghosts—become all that we are.

Drawing from his background as a youth addiction counselor, Dries provides a screaming rendition of what's at stake when we let our guard down. In turn, we're driven to dissect each tragic story until we've exposed the fragile humanity struggling to blossom within, a sentiment that echoes throughout "Tallow-Maker, Tallow Made." Here, a young woman suffers the sins of her father only to manifest something far more sinister by way of her yearning to have him back. And while some blossoms offer sustenance to fuel our caring desire, in the end, we find ourselves face to face with the ruin of our best intentions.

Bold and unflinching, Dries grabs us by the heart and hurtles us through a kaleidoscopic landscape of suffering. We're made to toe the line between blind faith and despair as evidenced in "Shadow Debt" when a kind old woman becomes hunted for saving a life all while forced to watch the love of her own life fade away piece by lonely piece.

With stories like "Damage Inc.," we experience the slow decay of sympathy through a woman who professionally impersonates the dead for any mourner tortured and wealthy enough to hire her. Meanwhile, the title entry, "Cut to Care," pays homage to a self-made savior eager to give anyone in need the literal skin off his back.

Expect to have your heart punched out as awful truths are splayed before your eyes ripe for critical contemplation. Not for the squeamish nor weak of mind. Then again, as the author's jagged little hurts so eloquently allude, neither is caring.

As you can see, there's a lot I left on the editing room floor, and for good reason. Some of my notes, while meant to capture my feelings in the moment, did nothing to help the reader understand what to expect from the book. That bit about the whole author orgy thing? Yeah, that might have helped me revisit how I felt, which was helpful to get back into the mood I had for Aaron's style, but it hardly served the review in any meaningful way even though I thought it was a pretty clever comparison.

This also might be a good time to mention that while we might be struck by a bit of genius and find ourselves writing the most profound bit of prose we've ever written, consider first and always: Does it serve the review and convey what a reader can expect from the book without taking the shine away from the book? In other words, are you writing to show off your writing or to showcase the writing of the author whose work you're reviewing? Maybe your instincts and general understanding of the task are better established than mine was when I first started writing reviews, but I for one used to use reviews as a way to show off my debatable mad skills. I would insert clever intros as if I were telling my own story within my review. After all, they should be entertaining, right? Well, sure, they shouldn't be boring, but you never want to make it about yourself no matter how clever or outstanding your prose might be. If a single word or sentence doesn't serve to accurately convey what a reader can expect to experience in the book you're trying to entice them to buy, then cut it out as fast as possible and forget it existed. Again, the review is not about you, it's about the book and its author.

LEAN, MEAN, AND CONCISE

W HEN I GOT my editing notes back on this guide, the wonderfully talented editor Dane Erbach suggested I add some concrete advice on how to actually trim the fat and how to write concisely. After all, I mentioned these two aspects of review writing earlier without going into details on how to do it. Of course, Dane is right. On reflection, telling you to be concise and make sure you trim the fat is like telling a toddler to "pay attention!" without teaching them what paying attention means. The last thing I want to do is have you put down this guide without having the clarity to fully understand how to pull off anything mentioned here. As with great storytelling, showing will always outweigh telling, so let me show you what I mean.

Because it's hard to separate being concise from trimming the fat, I'm going to discuss them in equal parts since you can't really have one without the other. By trimming the fat, those unnecessary bits of your review that don't do much, if anything, to convey your main points, you will naturally make your review a more concise representation of what you felt about a book. By focusing on the main points of your review, and homing in on exactly how to express your takeaway from a book, those unnecessary bits will either fall off the page with ease or won't get there in the first place. Clear as mud? Let me add a couple of examples to show you what I mean. As we go over the examples, I implore you to always keep one important thing in mind as you apply the following tips to your own writing: If you can take ten words and use a single word to replace them and still get your point across, do it. Always. (Those mini-review exercises can help with this.)

This first example of being concise and trimming the fat is from a book I reviewed called *Stephen King Revisited: Volume 1* by Richard Chizmar, with King historian Bev Vincent along with a slew of guest writers. Here's a paragraph from my first draft, in which I mention what the book's intention is.

As much a love letter to King's influence as it is an autobiographical roadway of Chizmar's profession and passion for words. Each segment presents another branch of road along the expressway which begins with King, and interchanges with his own style and direction, all of it leading to the present day with a collection of signposts commemorating each vital stop along the way. We are left with not only an immersive exploration into the works of King via his first 14 publications and the impact they made on the hearts and minds of some of the best pens scribing today

Before you scroll down the page to see what changes I made, take a moment to see if you can figure out why this doesn't quite work the way it is written. Take your time with it. Read it out loud. Does it flow naturally? Is it smooth? Does it place a clear image in your mind and clearly convey a specific message? Not so much, does it? This was written as a stream of conscience, and it shows. The sentences run as though they're chasing zebras in the jungle. They evoke images as clear as dirt and multiple bits are squeezed into a single gulp, making it difficult to know what to focus on.

How would you have written this differently? Do you see any opportunities to swap out a few words with one single one? Are there any thoughts that repeat themselves using different words which are ultimately redundant and unnecessary? Do you see any way to break up multiple ideas into a single, more easily digestible one?

With all that in mind, check out how I ended up revising that paragraph.

Armed with the support of literary critic and essayist Bev Vincent, along with several genre standouts like Chet Williamson, Brian Keene, and Josh Boone, Chizmar revisits the first fourteen published books by King, including a few by some guy named Richard Bachman. As much a love

letter to King's influence as it is an autobiographical roadway along the corridor of Chizmar's own life and passion for storytelling, each segment examines another mile of collected signposts commemorating vital stops along the way. Lessons were learned, fears were faced, and friends were made within the pages of King's multiverse.

I'm not trying to convince you that the second paragraph is so perfect it's beyond even further improvement, but comparing the two, I think you will find that while the first knew where it wanted to go, the second knew how to get there. Coincidentally, the second paragraph is only one word shorter than the first one, yet it is more succinct. The sentences are more on point and allow the reader to focus on one main point at a time. You'll also find I kept my description in the second paragraph far less vague than in the first. Whereas I first alluded to the type of authors who contributed to this book, I cleaned it up by then providing specific examples of who those other authors are. This gives the reader a clear image that is more easily remembered because it isn't cluttered with an overabundance of descriptions competing to make a singular point. The first attempt also pulls the reader off the path by causing confusion due to left-out details only hinted at. If a point about the book is worth mentioning, then assume it's worth giving an example of (spoiler-free, of course).

Sometimes, big differences can come from the smallest of adjustments. Take this next example of a review I did for Aaron Dries's collection *Cut to Care: A Collection of Little Hurts.*

Through a collection of outstanding nightmares (with an intro from Mick Garris), we can't help but inherit the markings of intense caring after being awarded with an assortment of scars that haunt like ghosts. Given enough time, these scars—these ghosts –become all that we are.

Kind of intriguing, I think. But boy is that a lot of imagery competing for your attention without much room to breathe. Reading it back, I decided I didn't need to mention Mick Garris. His intro to the collection is a sweet bonus, and I love his work, but it really has nothing to do with the book I'm reviewing. It's not worth bogging my review down, so I cut it out. I also wanted to break up the imagery a bit more to give it a chance to settle in the reader's mind before going on to the next point.

I ended up with this:

> **Through this outstanding collection of nightmares, we can't help but inherit the markings of intense caring. By the author's deft hand, our reward is a collection of scars that haunt us like ghosts we can never shed. Given enough time, these scars—these ghosts—become all that we are.**

The neat thing here is that both of these versions are exactly forty-six words. Even though I added as well as cut out some words, I still managed to pull off a much clearer sense of the points I was attempting to convey with my review. There's a lot to be said for breaking up your points with bite-sized pieces, even if you need an extra word for the sake of bridging the points so that they still come off flowing naturally.

The third and final example I'll give on this point is from my review of Philip Fracassi's novel, *Boys in the Valley*.

> **Elevating this book from being just another high-octane romp through hell, is Fracassi's elegant, often poetic, heartfelt details poured into each character no matter their role in the story. In particular, Peter's relationship with the kinder of the priests, Father Andrew, exemplifies the beauty of goodness dwelling in even the darkest of places which is worth saving at all costs. Unfortunately for Peter, his fellow orphan brothers, and the priests, the cost of protecting what they believe in most might not be something they're able to afford no matter how dire the consequences of watching it get snuffed out might be.**

Verbal diarrhea much, right? I happily sliced off twenty-five words from the above example because too much imagery/description in one sentence only leads to muddled clarity and lost impact. By now, you might be getting a better sense of what adjustments I need to make before having to scroll down to what ended up making it into the published copy. There were several bits that were filler at best. I mean, when I write, "heartfelt details poured into each character no matter their role in the story, do I really need to emphasize "in the story"? Where else would their roles be? It's a book review. Obviously, everything is being referred to the story. Then a bit later I write, "Unfortunately for Peter, his fellow orphan brothers and the priests . . . " So, basically everybody? Why not just say that? If you can summarize, summarize as I did here,

> **Elevating this book from being just another high-octane romp through hell are Fracassi's elegant, heartfelt details given to each character no matter their role. By example, Peter's relationship with Father Andrew exemplifies the sacred beauty of goodness to be found in the darkest of places. Unfortunately, the cost that must be paid to protect what they most believe in may not be enough to save them before the final wisps of light are forever snuffed out.**

I don't know about you, but I don't need to know, nor do I care, what size of shoe someone is wearing when their leg is being lopped off in the middle of a massacre in chapter one. The finer details don't always count, will almost certainly derail readers from the relevant points you're trying to convey, and should almost always be the first to be cut from your first drafts, especially if you're being held to a maximum word count.

DEVIL'S IN THE DETAILS

NOW THAT WE'VE touched on things to be removed in the final draft of a book review, let's focus on things you should add. This is where we'll take weak statements such as "I liked it a lot" and cultivate them into examples of why you liked them so that whoever's reading your review will know why they may like it, too.

Not to honk my own horn (much), but I am happy to say I don't get too many requests for feedback when submitting my reviews these days. When I do get a reply asking me to change something before publication, it's usually because I failed to expand on a detail for clarification, most often in the form of providing an example of why I felt a certain way. Let's face it: Reviews need clear details. As a writer, we want everyone who reads us to write about how great we are, how we terrified a reader, how we moved them emotionally, how we taught them so much about this or that. As a reader, however, it's simply not good enough to read a review that states something along the lines of, "This book was really good. It scared me a lot and taught me about monsters." From a reader's perspective, this doesn't mean squat. It's generic and doesn't convey what makes the book great, scary, or informative. And guess what? If a reader walks away from our review with nothing but a generic take on the book you just read and loved, guess which book they'll forget about while they're busy ordering the next book that intrigued them? Yup, the one you reviewed. I know that seems harsh because it is harsh. I feel it is also the reality of a well-crafted review versus one that is not well-crafted. But not to worry, because that's what we're here for—to help ensure you have all the tools you need to intrigue and influence fellow book lovers to check out the books you recommend.

Let's take a look at a perfect example of this.

Here's a review I sent to *Rue Morgue* magazine that I thought was solid and well-crafted. That was until the editor, Monica, requested that I provide examples where I mentioned, without context, of what folks could expect to learn from a book about the writing life by Jeff Strand. The book is called *The Writing Life: Recollections, Reflections, and a Lot of Cursing.*

Here's the first draft I sent to Monica. See if you can spot any areas that left you wanting more info or you felt were lacking something that might have given you a stronger desire to read the book.

The Writing Life packs a bevy of wisdom from the writer next door, the guy who always says hello or talks about the weather from over the fence while plotting murder under the most hilarious of circumstances. To be clear, this is not a how-to-write book. Instead, we're provided with a raw depiction of what it took for one writer to succeed on the heels of a twenty-year journey of compiled rejections, lost opportunities, and embracing the truth fish like the warm fuzzy care bear it most certainly is not. Strand's 50th book (released on his 50th birthday!) is the golden key given to unlock secrets of how the average wordsmith might someday tell their boss to kiss their loyal ass before writing off into the sunset forevermore.

A common thread connecting the wisdom of each page is how an accumulation of baby steps can lead to the freedom to write full-time provided you possess intent, consistency, and unwavering passion. A touch of madness doesn't hurt either. Write long enough, though, and you're bound to steer into inevitable rough patches of devastating self-doubt. But, have no fear because Strand's got your back. Personal anecdotes and tips galore demonstrate how to steady your course by highlighting some of the mistakes he made so you don't have to.

Holding nothing back about his struggles, missteps and misfortunes, Strand applies the same level of fearless honesty when describing his

many accomplishments and what it took to achieve them. He deftly illustrates how a journey of blood, sweat, and cursing is won by inches, not miles. Straightforward and entertaining as hell with plenty of laughs along the way, consider this book the well-crafted tool missing from your arsenal. It won't make your boss happy, but your writing life will thank you.

Did you notice anything missing? Any spots in the review where you thought, *What does he mean?* Places that felt flat? Monica did. She advised me to provide examples of lessons Jeff learned and flesh out the tips he demonstrates—lessons and tips that I merely hint at without backing them up.

Here's the final draft after incorporating a few tweaks. It made it a stronger review, and I think you can see the difference a couple of small changes can make to hammer the difference between telling a reader they should read something and actually showing them why they should read something.

The Writing Life packs a bevy of wisdom from the writer next door, the guy who always says hello or talks about the weather from over the fence while plotting murder under the most hilarious of circumstances. To be clear, this is not a how-to-write book. Instead, we're provided with a raw depiction of what it took for one writer to succeed on the heels of a twenty-year journey of compiled rejections, lost opportunities, and embracing the truth fish like the warm fuzzy care bear it most certainly is not. Strand's 50th book (released on his 50th birthday!) is the golden key for readers seeking to unlock the secrets of how the average wordsmith might someday tell their boss to kiss their loyal ass before writing off into the sunset forevermore.

A common thread connecting the wisdom of each page is how an accumulation of baby steps can lead to the freedom to write full-time provided you possess intent, consistency, and unwavering

passion. A touch of madness doesn't hurt either. Write long enough, though, and you're bound to steer into inevitable rough patches of devastating self-doubt. But, have no fear because Strand's got your back. Personal anecdotes and tips galore demonstrate how to steady your course by highlighting some of the mistakes he made and learned from such as succumbing to imposter syndrome or not intervening sooner when you know that improvised light shade is going to catch fire during your awards ceremony monologue.

Holding nothing back about his struggles, missteps, and misfortunes, Strand applies the same fearless honesty when describing his many accomplishments and what it took to achieve them. He deftly illustrates how a journey of blood, sweat, and cursing is won by inches, not miles. Straightforward and entertaining as hell with plenty of laughs along the way, consider this book the well-crafted tool missing from your arsenal. It won't make your boss happy, but your writing life will thank you.

To further exemplify how minor changes can make a big impact when crafting an effective review, here's a draft of a review I sent over to Monica at *Rue Morgue* for John Urbancik's book, *InkStained: On Creativity, Writing, and Art*. I also think this provides a cool glimpse into how a professional magazine editor can be an invaluable support system for further helping a reviewer to hone their craft and learn by doing the thing. It also demonstrates what a quality editor expects from a publishable review.

This is my first draft with notes from the editor:

Capturing the heart of John Urbancik's podcasts across 2017 and 2018, *InkStained* proves essential for any writer looking to hone their craft. Hell, it might even appease readers who find themselves asking, for the millionth time, where do writers get their ideas?

Reading through Urbancik's book is much like taking a long drive through the country while your favourite non-distracting music fills the air. Except backroads are replaced by memories of a writer who earned every one of them. Trees and the surrounding landscape are replaced by John's experiences and the car is fueled by his eagerness to share what he's picked up along the way for the benefit of you and I. [THIS METAPHOR ISN'T QUITE WORKING HOW YOU WANT IT TO, AND IS IN FACT MUDDYING THINGS UP, CAN YOU TRY SOMETHING ELSE HERE?]

Part how-to, part diary, part stream of thought, this is 100% Urbancik, and though he occasionally strays from his own beaten path, it's during these diversions that we truly get a glimpse of the writer's mind. It's almost as if the author graciously cracked open his skull, handed us a scalpel and told us to "have at 'er." In fact, this book takes such a deep dive into John's writing life and personal world at large [EXAMPLES, PLEASE], you'll probably want to roll over and smoke something when you're done.

While you are, of course, free to read *InkStained* at your own pace, you're also encouraged to put in some work. Scattered throughout the book are challenges designed to grease your creative gears. [CAN YOU ADD A COUPLE OF EXAMPLES OF THESE CHALLENGES?]

Although some passages do get hammered home a bit severely, most will have you re-reading to ensure that you've absorbed all of Urbancik's wisdom. For this reviewer, the book managed to spark one completed story and the outlines for two more. What will *InkStained* do for you? Your mileage may vary, but there are rewards in these pages all the same.

And here's the draft I sent back after putting Monica's suggestions into effect (which she was pleased with and published in the next issue of the magazine):

Capturing the heart of John Urbancik's podcasts across 2017 and 2018, *InkStained* proves essential reading for any writer looking to hone their craft. Hell, it might even appease readers who ask, for the millionth time, where writers get their ideas from.

Part how-to, part stream of thought, Urbancik describes his creative process with selfless abandonment. While occasionally straying from his own beaten path, it's during these diversions we glimpse the writer's mind. The author discusses everything from how to capture inspiration from a mundane job to how a focused day at the cemetery can spark the next published novel.

We get a sense of walking in the author's shoes as he discusses not only how to cope with the ongoing rush of creative traffic demanding to be heard, but how he personally thrives within it as a writer, an adventurer, and as a man. It's as if Urbancik graciously cracked open his skull, handed over the scalpel, and told us to "have at 'er." In fact, this book takes such a deep dive into John's writing life you'll probably want to roll over and smoke something when you're done.

And, while you're free to read at your own pace, you're also encouraged to put in some work. Designed to keep your creative gears greased are various challenges scattered throughout the book. From writing seven stories in seven days to self-care suggestions to sampling other art forms, prepare to lay waste to any excuses you might have for not getting more from your muse.

Although some passages do get hammered home a bit severely, most will have you re-reading to ensure you're absorbing as much of Urbancik's

wisdom as possible. For this reviewer, the book managed to spark one completed story and outlines for more. What will *InkStained* do for you? Your mileage may vary, but you don't want to miss finding out.

Although our job as reviewers isn't anywhere near as extensive as that of the authors we cover, I can't emphasize enough the importance of showing versus telling all the same as evidenced by the two examples above. I think it's worth noting—literally writing it down so as not to forget—that while readers will never know what you edited out or what you chose not to include, they will be affected by what you did write for better or for worse. You have to make every word count, and that means providing examples of why you felt a book worked or didn't work rather than simply stating it worked and moving on to the next sentence in your review. It's not good enough to say a book was suspenseful without telling us why. Perhaps the author was adept at foreshadowing things to come or establishing living, brooding atmospheres that could almost be heard creaking and groaning with every page turned; maybe the author rocked at developing characters that weren't quite right and who evolved in strange ways as the story went along. This requires you, the reviewer, to stretch yourself, really dig into the essence of the book, and consider what it was that made you step away with certain feelings about what you just read. If this sounds challenging for you, maybe even mission impossible, trust me when I say the more you practice, the easier it will be to nail down your feelings in a way that readers can't ignore as they read your personal takeaways.

REFLECTING TONE

THIS IS A good time to mention how I often try to mirror the overall mood and tone of a book in my review as a way to not only keep the process fresh and fun for me but also as a way to represent what a reader can expect from any given book I happen to review. After all, if it's the author's job to tap into their telepathy ability by bringing us into their world, then it's our job to be the conduit for their telepathy by being the portal through which the readers' senses become pulled into that author's world.

Of course, it's one thing to suggest capturing the tone of a book in your review, but it's another thing entirely to understand how to do it. In many ways, I feel like pulling it off is something I have developed over the years without really thinking about it. It's just something (I think) I've gotten better at the more I do it. But hey, this is a guidebook, and telling you the secret to capturing the tone in your review by saying something snazzy such as, "You gotta, like, just sort of feel it, man," not only sounds like some hippy-dippy mumbo jumbo garbage, but it also does nothing to serve you or this guidebook.

The first thing I consider when attempting to capture a specific tone in my review is this: What style did the author pull off in their book? Was humor a big factor? Was it primarily character-driven? Did the plot take a backseat to the imagery and descriptive prose? Or maybe it was a fun-filled monster tale with its only goal being to entertain you without much in the way of plot twists, character arcs, or poetic prose.

I recently reviewed a new collection from Eric LaRocca called *This Skin Was Once Mine*. Although Eric is a fantastic author with beautiful grotesque imagery in his writing, this collection of four novellas focuses on putting ordinary people into treacherous, often bizarre, and life-altering situations. As such, rather than spend my review discussing how the book made me feel or discussing the intricate plats of each novella, I instead focused on spotlighting the weird situations the characters found themselves in. I emphasized what was at stake for them, why it mattered that they should be in the situations they were in, and how effed up their situation truly was. My review had little to do with how I felt overall and instead focused on the specific experience of living inside the heads of these strange people as they led us into some very strange circumstances while I questioned my own comfort level throughout.

Meanwhile, when I reviewed Kristopher Trianna's novel, *That Night in The Woods*, the book made ambitious attempts to involve several characters who each had a unique backstory and set of motivations. No character made it to the end of this book without experiencing a major developmental arc. Because this novel had a complex plot with various branches that would ultimately intersect by the finale, my focus for the review was on the characters, on the plotlines, and how Trianna pulled off such a creepy tale involving so many relatable people.

Not only does doing our best to capture the tone of the book in our reviews help the reader get a better sense—they gotta feel it, man—of whether the book you're reviewing is for them or not by way of their attraction to the tone you're conveying, but it also goes a long way to keep things fresh for you. Imagine if all your reviews felt the same way. Now imagine if every author also came across using the same tone. It would get boring real quick, right? Not only do I feel strongly that working to set up proper tone in your reviews helps serve the book you're reviewing, but I believe it will also serve to keep you reviews fresh, fun, and challenging for as long as you continue to write them.

Digging a bit deeper into the value of conveying the right tonality, if a book was intense and dealt with extreme levels of terror, possibly in gory, graphic ways, then I'll try to match that by focusing my style more toward being intense and pointed. This will affect the language I use, which is not to say I will use lots of curse words (I usually avoid those anyway—that's just crass and seems schlocky to me), but rather I will use metaphors and examples that tend to be more on the harsher end of things. For stories like that, I focus more on offering examples of emotionally challenging scenes and talk about how the book is not for the faint of heart with examples of why.

On the flip side, if a book happens to be on the more humorous end of the spectrum, I'll be sure to follow suit in my review to the best of my ability. This doesn't mean I'm going to try extra hard to be funny (I think doing so will come across as phony and is likely not to land very well) and this isn't to say you should be trying to compete with the author of the work you're covering (reviews are always about the book and its author, never about you). What I'm trying to say is that if you can pull off demonstrating a similar style in your review as what is in the book, it will serve to capture what can be expected in the book as accurately as possible.

Here's an example of a review I did for Monster Matt Patterson's book *HA-HA Horror Collector's Edition*. I also think this review is a solid example of how to review a book which might not have been written entirely for you, per se, but one which you can still manage to find plenty to enjoy if not respect as far as what the author contributed to the genre.

The man of a thousand bad monster jokes is back with his latest installment of stunners and shunners. Running the full gamut of horror icons from *Dracula* to *Creature from the Black Lagoon*, *Basketcase* to *Slime City* and everything in between, no monster is immune to the tormented mashing of Patterson's zany antics. All manner of horror fare is fed through the demented joke-grinding device lurking in the depths of Matt's strange subconscious and spit out on the pages for your displeasure. You'll grimace, you'll chortle, you'll cry. Heck, you'll probably end up blowing milk out your nose and hug your knees pondering what you've gotten yourself into, and that's just the first chapter. Will you make it to the end before ripping your own funny bone out if only to beat yourself into oblivion with it? Consider yourself triple dog dared to try.

Each chapter is kept brief and lean, a small but courteous mercy from the author. As an allegory to Patterson's favourite monster movies, each chapter is introduced with a short history about whichever film is about to be mocked. A standout

for me are the few chapters showcasing Patterson's artwork which I found to be an enjoyable throwback to the gleefully macabre monsters I loved as a kid, complete, of course, with groan-worthy captions. As if knowing readers will inevitably seek out sharp objects by the book's conclusion, the collection also includes a section of dismembered monster parts to cut out and mix and match to your weird heart's content should you be so inclined.

As a special bonus, here's one not in the collection: what do you get when you cross this book with a sucker who'll try anything to remedy a nagging horror-comedy craving? Mental mutilation by a thousand puns. You're welcome.

Based on the tone of my writing and the phrasing I utilized here, I feel the reader will have an accurate idea of what to expect should they decide to pick up this book for themselves, whether they thank me for it later or not.

When it comes to tonality, to phrasing, and to language and the way you stitch it all together, using your unique voice is completely up to you. That's where your personal voice, your innate talent, your "youness," comes into play and makes you the only person who could write the reviews you do. That's the best part of reviewing, at least for me: knowing that my review has the ability to help lead a reader to a new favorite book or author simply because that reader responded to my unique way of writing a review, even if it's hard for me to consider my style as unique in any way.

I believe utilizing tone, both your own and that of the book you're reviewing, creates a type of magic that you and the reader will be better off capturing. Capture the what now? Sounds like some new-age mumbo jumbo hoopla, right? Let's take a closer look at what I mean before you judge me too harshly.

If you've read *On Writing* by Stephen King—which you totally should—then you might recall something interesting he said when discussing the writing process. Okay, everything he said in the book was interesting, but I'm thinking specifically of when he equated effective writing to the power of telepathy. Don't quote me on this, as it's been a few years since I last read this one, but essentially King stated that when you nail a scene, an event, a moment in your story just right, then whatever emotional state you were in while writing is the exact state your reader will be in when they read it. Write about the time you ran through the woods for your life as a ravenous man-eating beast was hot on your heels and guess what? Anyone reading your work will be transported to that exact forest with that exact beast with those exact fears as if they had run alongside you the entire way through. That's the magic. That's telepathy. That's the power of effective writing.

What better way to enable a reader to know they'll get as much from a book as you did than to create a portal they can step through to experience the book as you experienced it and to feel the same emotions and reactions as if they were there with you in spirit the entire way through? Create a well-crafted review, and that's exactly the impact you can have on a reader. That's the best. That's the magic. That's how you capture 'em and bring them in to pick up whichever book you review.

WHAT IT'S ALL ABOUT?

IF I WERE to end off this guidebook here, some of you might think I forgot to include something. We've reviewed reviews in more detail than you may have thought possible (me included). We covered stuff such as how to write a good hook and an intriguing conclusion, be concise, infuse relevant tonality, squeeze the most juice out of every book you read, and so on. But we haven't talked about including the plot, have we? Seems obvious to mention what a book is all about doesn't it? Well, does it? In a way yes, but for me personally, I don't put a lot of emphasis on it. After all, if a reader only wanted to know what the book is about, what the heck do they need us for? That's what a synopsis is for, something they can find with a few simple clicks, which will lead them to an Amazon store or publisher's site where they can read it and be on their way. Our job as I see it is to inform readers what the author has done with the plot.

Let's say we're reviewing the book about Jane chasing Spot. What does the author do to make us care about either Jane or Spot? Where does the author set this chase? What is keeping Jane from catching Spot? Why is Spot running from her in the first place? How does the author make me want to turn each page, mull over every word, and make me keep up with Jane until the end? And what, if anything, has been accomplished to make me think about Spot and all that chasing Jane did long after The End? That's the stuff I care about, and I think it's safe to assume that's the stuff readers care most about, too. Still, it doesn't hurt to at least have an idea of what a book is about, which is why I do include a summary of what it's all about—but the keyword here is *summary*.

If it helps, remember Stephen King once questioned why anyone would want to ruin a perfectly good story with plot. He wasn't talking about book reviews, but it certainly applies here.

When it comes to book reviews, we're doing our best to sell the sizzle, that alluring attraction that fires up the senses, so readers will want the steak or, in this case, the book. For some of us, summarizing plots in a tight way comes easy. For others, like me, it doesn't and will demand you practice it until it becomes as close to second nature as possible.

Remember those Grim Reader Reviews I mentioned earlier in this guide? Those are great practice for not only writing concise reviews in general but summarizing the plot like you've never summarized before. When sixty words are all you've got, you better make every word count as though each one written represented ten. This practice especially comes in handy when you're introducing readers to a new book that's half a dozen books deep in a series. I love me an engaging series, so I've been in this situation a few times and, with practice (and learning how other reviewers better than me have done it), I like to think I've gotten adept at it enough to show you a sample.

In this example, I reviewed *DarkWalker: Other Realms* by John Urbancik. This was the sixth and final book in the series. While each book wasn't overly long, a helluva lot happened in the five books that came before. Likewise, I had a helluva time trying to summarize the series up to that point without feeling like I was doing it an injustice; I didn't want to leave out vital parts or reveal any spoilers. Plus, I also had to make sure the reader didn't feel like whatever I had to say about *Other Realms* was lost on them because they didn't have any references to the previous books in the series.

Here's what I ended up with for my review of *Other Realms* in *Rue Morgue* magazine's Jan/Feb 2021 issue #198:

From the time Jack Harlow was kissed by a ghost, he's walked untouchable observing the creatures of the night. Succumbing to a reclusive life among shadows, he never expected to meet his soul mate, Lisa Sparrow, who sacrificed everything to protect him when a torrent of nightmare beasts threatens to decimate the living.

As a DarkWalker, Jack has traversed various levels of hell, uncovered secrets of his origin, battled through fabled silver mines, and fought

Gods on the mountain Armageddon while absorbing the strengths and abilities of each creature encountered.

NOTE: This next previous paragraph in particular is where I put my summarizing magic to work, taking a few words of description from each book. This way, I can tie in where the series has been into where the series has gone with this newest installment.

Now, after a devastating war in Shangri La, Jack reawakens in a spirit realm where he meets an immortal woman of legendary beauty. Following ethereal threads only Jack can see, they're led into yet another realm where the DarkCrawler, an all-powerful evil entity, lures Jack into a final showdown to rid the universe of its DarkWalker once and for all.

Neither hero nor anti-hero, Jack thrives in the layers of grey between as the balance the universe doesn't know it needs. Most striking is how deftly Urbancik derives the humanity from his monsters and the monsters from his humanity. Like a maestro possessed by the devil himself, Urbancik orchestrates a rending combination of beautifully dark prose that cuts to the point. Fantastic images reverberate beyond each word, laced with a deep sense of wonder that's rife with elements of hope, sorrow, and reconciliation.

The epic journey draws to a frenzied crescendo guaranteed to rip your heart out, set it ablaze, and shove its smoldering remains back into your heaving chest, altered forever. While best read in chronological order, jump in anywhere you can. Considering each book's re-readability, you'll likely revisit the world of the DarkWalker if only to better understand what may be lurking within your own dark shadows.

A REVIEWER'S GUIDE TO WRITING BOOK REVIEWS

For practice, think of a series you've read. Now think of a few words you might use to describe each book. Now use them to write a summary of the series. Can you do it in a dozen or so words? Keep trying until you do, and you will be amazed at how you can say so much with so little.

This same approach to summarizing a series can also fall in line with summarizing collections or anthologies. When working within a specific word count and a reader's attention span, it's impractical to discuss every story you read in a collection. I tend to give a few examples of the stories to make my point about the general vibe and execution of the book, using just a few words to summarize whatever story I'm using as my example. This creates room for the reader to "sample" the book without the need to slog through each story description before deciding whether to buy it.

Speaking of samples, I don't know about you, but sometimes when I am done reading a particularly enjoyable book, my immediate inclination is to tell everyone I know who might also enjoy the book everything about it. I want to tell them exactly what makes a book great. My second inclination is to zip my lips because who wants a good book spoiled, right? Now, if you're tasked to review the book, sometimes it's tough to summarize without giving too much away, especially if you're trying to avoid simply repeating the synopsis. Sometimes, we might even give a little of the meat away without realizing it. I've done it myself. One time, while describing an exciting plot point I felt would give an example of the intensity in store for readers, I gave a surprise away. The author called me out on it (in a nice way, which is also why I like to give authors a peek at my review before I send it off), and I adjusted my review to warn readers of the mild spoiler ahead.

Personally, I don't recommend spoilers no matter how mild they may seem. If you must include them for whatever reason (you may deem it necessary to make a point, for example) make sure you give the reader a heads up and warn them ahead of the spoiler. That said, I think it works best to leave the surprises for the reader to experience organically, same as you got to. I also think describing your experience of the book without spoilers takes more effort; spoiler-ridden reviews tend to be a lazy way out and risk turning readers off of the books you're trying to promote, which is probably not your intention.

By this point in our coverage of writing book reviews, you may have noticed an elephant in the room. Maybe you only felt it, maybe you only suspected it, maybe you and the elephant shared a few awkward glances while pretending neither of you noticed the other one. Either way, we need to talk about this. It's the very thing that seems to get the most polarizing opinions on social media and hushed circles around the globe, certainly within our industry where opinions vary as wildly as our tastes in the books we love. I am, of course, referring to bad book reviews. No, not poorly written ones—we're all here to write great reviews to the best of our abilities. I'm referring to reviews of books that just didn't work in any meaningful way for the reviewer for any number of reasons. Surely, you've seen them before? Those scathing reviews that all but scream at you to stay away from this steaming pile of dung lest you get some on you never to be the same again. Some of them go so far as to question why the author even bothered to get up in the morning to write such drivel when they should have joined a bowling league with the time they spent scratching at paper. Welcome to cancel culture folks, where someone can work their ass off to write the best book they can write after months of pouring their hearts out over their laptops only to have the masses tell them they should have been, well, anything else but the writer they always dreamed of.

Is there merit to writing a bad review that you detested like last week's leftover meatloaf? Does it provide any value to you, the author, the publisher (assuming it wasn't self-published), or to you and anyone who might read your scathing review? Again, opinions about all those questions are as varied as the books in a library. My opinion is that they don't do anything worth spending time on. Whenever I read a scathing review, I'm forced to judge the reviewer's value of their own time. Seriously, who has time to read books they loathe? Life is too short to read bad books, and with so many books to choose from, why not DNF the book and go on to something else? Why waste time trudging through it just so you can tell other readers how bad it was? You know the best way to share how bad you thought it was? With silence. By not giving the book the time of day nor shining any light on it, you'll inadvertently make it tougher to be discovered by readers who probably prefer hearing about books they might like as much as you did.

Now don't get me wrong. This isn't to say that you if you liked a book for the most part but felt any aspects of it fell flat for you or simply weren't well done, by all means, mention it briefly. But do your best to keep the spotlight on what did work for you, what you did enjoy about the experience reading that book, and why and who you feel would also be apt to enjoy it. Your mileage may vary, but I'll always consider reviews as a way to help promote books I love so that others can enjoy them in as close to equal measures as possible. There's enough hate and anger brimming in the world and overflowing onto our social media feeds, don't you think? Sure, some authors share especially bad reviews in which it would seem their book truly ruined somebody's day, but I assure you it is all in jest because that author has chosen to laugh it off and is sharing it as a joke to further promote their book. Heck, sometimes some of the angriest reviews happen to be folks who apparently stumbled onto an extreme horror book when clearly, extreme horror is not for them. In those cases, hearing about how awful and twisted and vile a book is might actually be a great selling point for those who are looking for such reading experiences. The point is that if a book is badly written, you're better off moving on to another book that's worth your time to celebrate and review. If, however, the book is well enough written but left you feeling meh about it, consider if the book was really for you and if there are any good points worth mentioning to someone who may find what was meh for you is a plus for them.

Remember the review I exampled earlier about the punny monster jokes? Sure, it wasn't a book written solely to my tastes, but I was able to recognize and mention its strong points and the areas that I did in fact enjoy. I also think I conveyed the zany tone of the book well enough in my review that readers were likely to know what to expect so that those who gave the book a chance, would come away having their expectations met.

The final point I'll make here before I feel like I am simply beating a dead cow with a stick is that if you feel you must write a negative review about the book you just read, consider what you want to get out of writing it, what you want readers to get out of reading your review, and what value the author and their publisher might get out of having such a review accessible to potential readers. Then ask yourself: Is it really worth it? Who am I helping? Let your answer be your guide.

YOU WROTE A REVIEW!

NOW WHAT?

ORGET ABOUT THE cheeky chapter title for a moment. Seriously, writing a review, like writing anything creative, is something many talk about doing but few in fact do. If you happen to be one of the few who took an ambition and followed it up by applying ass to chair, fingers to keyboard or pen, then good on you. The first step is often the toughest and nobody ever got good at anything they didn't practice. In other words, congrats on accomplishing the most important step in the process of becoming a reviewer.

But now that you've got a review written, what the heck do you do with it?

Well, if you have a personal blog, then it's time to get blogging, you reviewer you! Post your review to that blog, and be sure to include a cover pic. When it comes to snagging people's fleeting attention online, a picture goes a long way to reeling in all the juicy eyeballs you can handle. So put the book cover front and center of your review or at least beside your review where it can be easily seen, and let people know at a quick glance which book you're telling them about before you even begin telling them about it. You'll also want to include a link for readers to purchase whatever book you just got them excited to read. Following up with a short author bio isn't necessary, but that's a personal choice. If you think readers need to know what else an author may have written or if they have won any awards, then go ahead and mention it. Otherwise, your review on its own is fine and dandy.

Oh, you don't have a blog? No sweat. As of this writing, several friends and colleagues have informed me you can post book reviews on Amazon without having had to purchase the book, which is great if you happened to get an ARC sent to you for free

A REVIEWER'S GUIDE TO WRITING BOOK REVIEWS

by an author or publisher. I say as of this writing because anything can and often does change at a moment's notice, and who knows if Amazon will change its mind about this. Until then, go ahead and post your review on the author's Amazon book page, and feel free to send it to them so they can share it with the world if they choose to do so. Posting favorable reviews really helps Amazon know which books are most likely to be picked up and bought; if the algorithm detects that readers are responding positively to the book, it will suggest the book to more readers.

One note of caution, though. If you happen to leave a five-star review, make sure the book warrants it as one of the best books you read in your life and you can't imagine how the book could have been written any better. Which isn't to say a book you review may not warrant five stars, just keep in mind that Amazon gets a bit suspicious if a book has too many five-star reviews and may think readers are working together to inflate that book's quality. Likewise, too many one-star reviews and Amazon starts to think a nasty group of angry people are out to sabotage a book's success (whether they actually read the book or not). Generally, Amazon will average out the reviews between the two- to four-star ranking so their algorithms can push the book in front of potential buyers accordingly. Again, if the book warrants five stars, by all means, rank it accordingly. It's just good to understand how the algorithm works. Alternatively, if the book warrants a one-star review because you can't imagine how a book could give you any worse of a reading experience, then, well, you might want to skip the effort of reviewing it because words are hard and even bad books took time and effort for someone to create. Probably best in that case to just quietly move on to a book you may enjoy more and respond to with a bit more enthusiasm.

But wait a minute—you want to publish your review in a print or online publication that you and everyone on the planet can access in all its glory? I may have a few ideas to help you do exactly that.

This is the part where I describe how I first got to see my reviews getting published with another reminder that my experience is my experience, and yours is yours. I'll let you know a few places to consider as far as where to start pitching your stuff to, but keep in mind these are merely suggestions. You might (and I hope you do) find even more places to set your sights on than I did.

As I mentioned way back at the start of this whole thing, I began writing reviews when I wrote one for Jack Ketchum's *Only Child*. Since *Insidious Reflections* had sadly closed their doors, I heard through the grapevine (likely from one of those early newsgroups) about a review site called *Hell Notes*. I honestly can't remember if somebody referred me to the site or not, but I kinda think someone must have. At any rate, I let them know I had been writing for *Insidious Reflections* for most of their issues and I was looking for a place to publish my review of *Only Child*. They invited me to send along my review and then published it on the site. They didn't (and still don't) pay for reviews but, hey, I could officially call myself a published book reviewer, so what did I care? Plus, it was online, so I could easily post up links and direct folks to check it out. I would go on to publish several books and movie reviews with them over the next several years. *Hell Notes* is a great place because they are constantly getting books sent to them from publishers looking for reviews. Each month I would get a list of books up for review, and it was simply a matter of picking which book I would like to review and wham bam, I had a book to review and a place to publish it.

Goodreads can also be a fine place to post your review. Here, you can find almost any book published—literally thousands of books from thousands of authors from all walks of genre—and users regularly review their favorite reads. Go ahead and join them. I will admit that while I do have a Goodreads profile (they're free, so why not?), it is not a platform I spend much time on, mostly likely to my detriment. While I can't give you a deep dive into the pros and cons of this platform, I can tell you it can be a wonderful place to get your review seen by those readers who can benefit from it. It's also a platform that is certainly getting a lot more attention from publishers looking to market their books as widely as possible.

Speaking of publishers, many of them have blogs discussing various books, post interviews, and other media plugs from around the net. If you just wrote a review, it might not be a bad idea to dig around a book publisher's website to see if they have a blog. If so, let them know you have just reviewed their book by Author McAuthorson and ask if they would like to publish it on their site or blog.

Generally, when it comes to finding blogs and various

publications to publish your reviews, Google will be your best friend. Those publications that don't pay may not pay because they are small, new, underfunded, or all of the above. And as much as I would love to say, "Here's a giant list of all the publishers you need to know about! Now go forth and publish much!" sadly, so many smaller publications come and go with the wind, not always through any fault of their own. Making money as a publisher is even tougher than trying to make money as a reviewer. For every site that has published my reviews that are still kicking today, such as *Hell Notes*, there are at least a dozen more that no longer exist. Hence, I suggest utilizing online searches with keywords such as "publication," "review," and whichever genre you happen to be reviewing. Social media is also a great way to solicit the hive mind and ask if anyone knows of publications looking to publish reviews.

Contacting publishers can be nerve-wracking if you've never done it before, but most sites make it easy to locate an email or use a form to make your enquiry. Plus, most don't bite, so the best thing is to not overthink the process (as I am apt to do from time to time) and keep your enquiry short, concise, and professional. Some publishers may want to see samples of your reviews, especially if it is a larger, paying publisher such as *Rue Morgue* or *Fangoria*. Lucky for you, you've got a handful of reviews you've already written and published on various blogs, Amazon, and author sites, right? Okay, while that last part was a bit cheeky of me, there's also a reason I suggested where to start, but keep in mind, the path is all your own and wherever you start is up to you. If you want to skip blogs, Amazon review sections, your Facebook posts, and so on, then by all means, shoot for the top and submit to the larger, paying publications. Just know it will be a bigger hill to climb, so prepare accordingly.

So, what the heck do you say to a publication or editor with whom you want to publish your reviews? Again, keep it as simple as possible. If you know which specific editor your message is going to, be sure to use their name. Going with Mr. or Ms. is always a safe bet. If you don't know their name because maybe you're using a form letter on their site, then a simple "Hello" works fine. An example might go as follows:

> *Hello, I'm writing to pitch you a review I wrote for Scary*
> *Story by Author McAuthorson. The book is coming out*

next month, and I feel it is one your readers would very much enjoy as it deals with relatable characters struggling through supernatural terrors that keep readers on the edge of their seats throughout the book. If you feel you can use my review for publication in Name Of Publication, then I will be happy to send it along right away.

Thank you for your time and consideration. I look forward to hearing from you.

Warm regards,
Reviewer McReviewerson

That's pretty much the same approach I take whenever I reach out to a publisher I want to send a review to if I have not contacted them previously. Feel free to alter it to suit your personality, but it's a great place to start. Just remember there's a chance you'll get a response rejecting your pitch for one reason or another. It happens, no matter how long you've been doing this for and no matter how prolific you may be. It's part of the gig and always will be. It's okay. Take the rejection and move on. It could be just a matter of timing. Remember, some publishers are already working on their issue two or three months ahead of time to ensure the next issue is always ready to go when needed. That's just how the business works. If you happen to pitch a review for a book that just came out or maybe has already been out for a month or so, there's a chance the review has already passed its "expiration date," so to speak, depending on the publishing cycle you're trying to be a part of. This is why I am so appreciative of authors who give plenty of advance notice when their books will be out, but more on that later.

Of course, every publication is different, so it's a good idea to familiarize yourself with as many of them as you can so you can best align your reviews and expectations accordingly. For example, *Cemetery Dance* online is happy to take older titles for review so they always have some they can keep on deck for when they might be a bit short any given week. While they only pay $10 USD for their reviews (more if you can get one into their print magazine), they can be an excellent place for posting books you didn't get to review until on or after the publication date of the book as well as a great home for any author interviews you might have (more on interviews later, too).

In case you're reading this and feeling either overwhelmed or slightly dejected because you can't seem to get your reviews into your most desirable publications, let me share a little story about the time I finally got a review published in my favorite magazine. Worth celebrating, right? At first it was, until it wasn't.

Let me explain.

In 2006 I went to an author reading in Toronto, Ontario (it was a 666-themed event on June 6th) where I met the book editor of my favorite genre magazine, *Rue Morgue*. After a tour of their fantastic headquarters the next day, I mentioned I had just read a hilarious zombie novel by a well-known author most readers of *Rue Morgue* would be familiar with. She told me to send a review along since it just so happened that she had a review fall through and had space in the magazine to fill. So, I slapped one together and sent it her way.

Look, I'm just going to fast forward this part and simply tell you the review I sent was a bit of a stinker but, because it was the final hour before the magazine was scheduled to go to the printer and every space had to be filled, my review went out with the magazine. I should have been stoked to finally have my review appear in my favorite magazine, right? A small part of me was. However, most of me was ashamed that a review that I was told was not up to a *Rue Morgue* level was going to be seen by readers worldwide whether it sucked or not. The review editor did their best to salvage the review and added a few changes which made it more publishable than it was. Still, it was not a good feeling knowing my review needed to be better and that I had likely blown my opportunity.

Thankfully, one of the reasons I am writing this guidebook is because I didn't totally blow my opportunity, but I certainly did get put in place. These days, I understand the work it takes to produce a review worthy of seeing print in a major publication. It was a sharp blow to my ego, but mostly it was a huge downer in that I felt like I had disappointed the magazine I wanted to impress so much. I vowed not to let that happen again, even if the path ahead just got a bit longer.

SHOW 'EM WHAT YA GOT OR NOT?

ONCE YOUR REVIEW has been completed, whether finalized to be published on your blog, in an ezine, or in a printed magazine, you may wonder if you should share it with the author or editor of whose book you just covered. Personally, the only time I don't share my reviews with authors and editors is if I simply don't have their direct contact information.

That isn't to say that you must share, but here's why I do it.

First, it just seems like a nice thing to do. It's my way of saying, "Hey, here's what I thought of your book, and I want you to check it out before anyone else as my way of saying thanks for writing/editing it." I've shared too many reviews to count, and I've yet to get a single negative response. Authors, publishers, and editors are generally happy to get a sneak peek. In some instances, they have been able to correct me on the spelling of a name or place I may have gotten wrong, thus saving me the embarrassment of seeing the mistake go to publication, a.k.a. the land of no return. Occasionally, I've had parts of my review used as blurbs on the books I've received early enough for blurbs to make it onto the final copy of the published book, which never fails to be very cool.

So yeah, at least from my experience, it's always been worth it to share my reviews. Should you do the same? It's entirely your call, but I would certainly recommend it. Plus, anything you can do to help further support a good relationship with editors, authors, and publishers can only help to benefit all parties involved.

DOUBLE DIPPING (TRIPLE DIP IF YOU MUST) FOR BEST RESULTS

IF YOU HAVE seen *that* episode of *Seinfeld*, then you know that double dipping is not to be trifled with. You just don't do it. Reviews, on the other hand, have no rules about how many times you get to dip a finished review into another opportunity. The point is that if you can write a review and get an opportunity to squeeze even more projects from the book you just read, especially if one or more of those squeezes gets you paid, then do it. You owe it to yourself to make the best of every book you read and if you ask me, the author and publisher can only benefit further from this.

Let me explain by reminiscing on a multiple dipping experience that is a perfect example of my point.

I've had the privilege of reviewing Gauntlet Press books more than any other publisher since I first began reviewing. I developed a pretty good relationship with its owner Barry Hoffman over the years, which I maintain to this day. On top of the many specialty releases he did, Barry also happens to be a fantastic author himself, so I also reviewed several of his books. A few years ago, Barry published a book called *Hope and Miracles: Two Screenplays from Frank Darabont (Shawshank Redemption and The Green Mile)*. I was happy to review a digital ARC of the book and Barry agreed to be interviewed and talk about the production of such an important book. I took a chance and asked if Frank Darabont might be willing to have me interview him. I'll spare the details and simply tell you that after much chasing down (as was the custom if one wished to communicate with Frank), he agreed to be interviewed over the phone and called me so we could do just that. It was a cool experience, to say the least, and one that would open

RICK HIPSON

a big ass door for me. You see, Gauntlet often did collaborations and would allow some of their titles to go to other publications to cross-promote books and help sell to a larger audience. One of the publishers Gauntlet collaborates with is Cemetery Dance. Barry put me in touch with Cemetery Dance owner Richard Chizmar, who was happy to have me send over my conversations with Frank and with Barry, as well as my review of the *Hope and Miracles* book. Not only was I able to publish these pieces on their site ($50 USD per interview and $10 USD for the review), but they also contracted me to have them published in an upcoming issue of Cemetery Dance magazine (about $360 USD). I've since published a third interview on *Cemetery Dance* with Tyson Blu, the editor of the *Hope and Miracles* book. On top of that, I recently caught the attention of another publisher for a collection of my reviews and interviews once it's completed, and my chat with Frank Darabont likely clinched that deal. Not to mention, that one book opened up the doors to Cemetery Dance for publishing many more reviews and interviews over the years (all with payments) along with a weekly interview column I never would have had a chance to publish with them had I not attempted to take that one book review one step further.

So, what do I think of double dipping? Is that all you've got? Dip that sucker for all you're worth. If your goal is making a professional go of your writing, then you owe it to yourself to be as prolific as you can with each and every opportunity you come across in your journey.

Obviously, mileage will always vary, and I have yet to have such a lucrative dipping session from a single book since *Hope and Miracles*, but I have had several book reviews turn into paid interview opportunities.

Does this mean you should only dip that book as often as you're getting paid to do so? That will always be your call based on your personal goals. That said, I really don't see how doing so, whether you get paid or not, has any disadvantages assuming it's not taking you away from anything you feel might give your time more value. I recall a book I reviewed quite early on in my journey. While I don't recall how I got the heads up for this book, Brian Keene published a signed, limited chapbook called *The Resurrection and The Life* which was published by Biting Dog Press in 2007. The co-owner, Dave Dinsmore was an awesome guy who loves books as much as we do, so when I asked him if I could interview Brian, he was happy to hook that up. Pretty sure that was the first time Brian and I chatted; we've stayed in touch over the years, and it all started with that one book, born of my choice to double dip for the added value of a new connection to one of my favorite authors and people. In fact, I ended up triple-dipping this book because I also got to do an interview with the illustrator, a fellow Canadian named George Walker, a fascinating artist who created unique wood blocks that he hand-engraved and stamped into the books. I've also had the chance to interview George for another book he collaborated on a few years ago; I chatted with him and author Martin Llewellyn to discuss *Necronomicon* released from Biting Dog Press. This was such a cool experience because not only did I get paid $100 USD for that review and subsequent interviews but, instead of the usual ARC, I was gifted one of only 35 very limited copies of the book along with a sweet handmade card which George created out of paper he made. Sometimes this reviewing thing pays off in very cool, unexpected ways. This story reminds me that it's not always about getting paid in cash, though that's a nice bonus when it happens, of course.

So, there you have it, that's my way of saying if you want to take reviewing seriously, then say "yes" every chance you can, and don't be afraid to ask authors and publishers if they would like to be interviewed along with you reviewing their book. Not only is interviewing a fun and informative way to learn about what goes on behind the scenes and in the minds of our favorite creators, but it's also an excellent way to grow your network of authors, publishers, and books for future consideration. I've never done an interview I regretted, and I'm sure the same will hold true for you, too. And let's face it, podcasts are getting more popular all the time, so much so that even YouTube has added a podcasts category to their uploads to make them easier to find on their platform. Anything you can do to help promote the work you love will only add value to what you do and to those creators who entrust you to help cover their work. Connecting with authors by way of reviewing their books has kept me in the loop for their upcoming releases, not to mention I get to call many of them friends after all these years.

Of course, it's not all smooth sailing. Like all reviewers, I have experienced bumps, disappointments, and occasional embarrassment along the way, all of which I have learned from. I like to think some lessons were learned through unavoidable errors on my part, so I wrote the next section to help you learn from them in the hopes you might avoid them along your journey and enjoy a slightly smoother experience—although don't forget that a few bumps in the road will be unavoidable.

Go ahead and grab a snack, pour a drink, take a trip to the 'loo or what have you. I'll see you back in the next chapter.

LIGHTS! CAMERA! MAKE A VIDEO?

I N CASE YOU thought interviewing authors was the only way of enjoying some added benefits as a reviewer, there is another option you may not have considered but it's worth being aware of: why not make a video?

It's no secret that platforms like TikTok, Instagram, and YouTube are growing exponentially year by year and competing with streaming services as the normalized method of consuming content, be it for entertainment, news, or general "how-to" education. Among the endless topics, dedicated creators discuss movies and books they love. So why not you? Making videos can be a super accessible option to do either instead of written reviews or alongside them. There will always be a need for written reviews for websites and magazines, but video reviews are a fun way to reach out to those who prefer their content in moving picture form they can digest on social platforms they are already immersed in. The great thing about making videos is the barrier to entry has never been thinner. Type in BookTok or Bookstagram, for example, and be amazed at how much promotional book content pops up. Don't have a full-scale studio in your back office? No problem. All you need to get started is your cell phone and a decent microphone you can buy for under a hundred bucks. If you discover a love for making videos, you can always upgrade your tech within your budget as you advance in your journey. (Pro tip: Whereas most viewers can forgive poor video, poor audio will never be your friend, so be sure to get the best mic you can afford.)

Some of you reading this might be terrified of putting your face online for all the world to see. If that's you, the good news is you don't need to. Plenty of creators produce faceless content and still do exceptionally well. And speaking of doing well, not only can making review-based book reviews attract and delight a new, wide-reaching demographic above and beyond the written word, it can also add an additional source of revenue, should you choose to put the work in. And believe me, if you think learning how to craft well-received book reviews that publications want to give you money for is hard, making profitable review videos is a whole other world. No, I'm not trying to scare you away, but I feel I do need to keep things real and explain that if you want to explore this arena with your reviews, then it's best you prepare yourself for a new chapter of learning, struggling, and growing as a capable reviewer. If you find the added workload and learning curve to be an enjoyable endeavor you're willing to fully embrace, then the personal, professional, and financial rewards can be truly awesome and game-changing for you. Growing a video audience organically (meaning without the temporary assistance of buying viewers and subscribers) by creating engaging videos that book lovers can't get enough of, can eventually be monetized with ad sense, affiliate marketing programs, and sponsorship deals to name but a few avenues of revenue.

Sweet, you say. Tell me more, you ask. Well . . . this is the part where I confess my own lack of expertise when it comes to making significant income by growing an audience using social media platforms. In fact, this is something I am currently learning and growing and struggling with myself. While I can assure you, that I absolutely love it as a means to reach a wider audience for the sake of boosting the signals on the authors and books I love, I'm still a ways off from going full-time and only making videos as my main source of cash, which is my eventual goal, but I digress. Enough about me. This is your review guide.

The awesome thing about the way the creator economy has been growing over the years is that there are so many channels and creators dedicated to making videos about how to grow with your topic of choice using platforms like TikTok, YouTube, etc. I encourage you to seek out as many of these channels as you can within your preferred platform(s) and watch them all until you find a few creators you enjoy learning from. Then consume as much of their content as you can and learn as much as you can while applying what you pick up. When I started on YouTube, for example, I typed in how to grow my review channel, and other such keywords like "podcast interviews," "grow my YouTube audience," and so on. I scoured the results and watched at least a dozen different creators until I narrowed down a few I found that resonated most for me. In case you're wondering or need a specific place to start, the main creators I watch most often are Nick Nimmin, Nate Black, Roberto Blake, Pat Flynn, Pod Sound School, and Vid IQ. I'm sure you'll discover your own favorites, but I think these are a great place for anyone to start learning some great concepts about growing a review channel—or any other channel.

Interests and results will always vary, but my focus when it comes to video reviews (and author interviews) has been on YouTube. It's my preferred platform, and you may find you prefer another, although don't ever feel you have to choose between this platform or that platform when choosing both platforms is always an option. However, my best advice is to stick with whichever one or ones you enjoy the most so long as it adds (rather than takes away) value and satisfies whatever goals you've set as a reviewer. The important thing is to be aware that other options are always there should you choose to explore them. Just make sure that whatever you choose, you choose it deliberately while making sure you can be consistent without getting burned out by taking on too much, which I can assure you is very easy to do if you allow it to happen.

For me, my only regret after all the time, energy, and effort I've spent growing my audience on YouTube over the past couple of years is that I didn't do it sooner. Will it be the same for you? There's only one way to find out. As long as you follow your passion and enjoy the journey, whatever path you choose has the potential to be a rewarding one. Just be clear on what those rewards need to look like for you to make it all worth it.

No matter what you decide to do with your reviews—be it making videos, posting on your blog, on Amazon, or publishing in printed magazines—I look forward to seeing what you create and where your reviews might take you.

REVIEW ETIQUETTE AND OTHER UNSPOKEN RULES

MOST OF THE STUFF I'll be mentioning here is common sense stuff, but maybe some of it isn't. At worst, it gives you a sense of some of the things you might come across in your journey and what you could do given the same scenario.

Contacting authors for the first time can be a bit daunting, though I assure you most of them are awesome people who are usually happy to hear from enthusiastic reviewers who appreciate their work. They are also busy people, too; they have their own lives to live and their own set of responsibilities and goals to worry about.

For example, I once solicited an author to review their upcoming book. This was about 10 years ago (had to look it up because I could have sworn it was only a few years ago. Sigh). At the time, I was publishing reviews and interviews pretty regularly through *Hell Notes* and felt my reviews were well-received. I also had a blog on which I would repost content, and overall thought I was doing a decent job. When I saw an announcement about an upcoming book by this author, I contacted him via social media. Although I'm not naïve or delusional enough to think I'm even close to being well-known among our community now, I was even less so back then. That said, I was sure this author had at least heard of me and was aware I always did my best to represent our mutual colleagues. In my message, I explained I have always wanted to review his work and if he was willing to send me an ARC then I would review it for *Hell Notes* which, as far as I knew, got plenty of eyeballs and I would also post it to my blog as well as interview him if he was willing and available. I don't remember his exact reply, but essentially, he responded with a polite no and cited his reasoning as being that he wanted his book reviewed on a bigger platform than I was suggesting.

To be honest, I was caught off guard, and my immediate reaction was to feel disappointed and a bit offended. I mean, I wasn't exactly shiny new at this point, and *Hell Notes* had been around for quite a while and had a solid reputation. I felt like it was fair to want your book reviewed on a big platform, but shouldn't an author want it on as many platforms as possible? Especially when a digital ARC costs nothing to send. What the hell, right?

While I may have had every valid reason to have felt the way I did, the bottom line is that the author I contacted clearly had other plans, and that's perfectly acceptable. For all I knew, his book at the time may have not been formatted as a digital ARC. Maybe he only had physical ARCs to send out (which are expensive to make and ship, especially internationally), and he may have wanted to get the best bang for his (and his publisher's) buck with every ARC sent out. Of course, I only considered all of this after the fact, and I'm glad I did because feeling jaded by a rejection to review a book should not change my life or yours. Does it suck? Sure. All rejections suck. But it's wise to remember that authors owe us absolutely nothing, and if they don't want us to review their book for any reason, that's a call they get to make no matter how we feel about it. Of course, if I REALLY wanted to review the book, I could have bought it online and reviewed it after reading it that way, which I've done for some other books. In this case, I simply moved on to the next book I was entrusted to review.

For the most part, authors are more than happy to have you review their work. But please, for the love of all things written, if you say you are going to review their work, then you owe it to them to do your best to review their work. Imagine putting all your sweat, heart, and tears into a book you toiled over for three months or more; finally, you have found someone interested in reading it and sharing it with the world, and then . . . nothing. Even if you're the only reviewer out of many to drop the ball on a review, well, that's still a crappy thing to do. Hey, I get it. Life happens. Things come up that throw our best intentions off the rails sometimes. But if for any reason you find yourself unable to review a book you promised an author you would provide in exchange for an ARC, then at least be sure to let the author know as soon as possible. Hopefully, they will be understanding and consider sending you an ARC in the future. What I can tell you with certainty is being timely and honest is always best practice no matter what.

Recently (as of this writing) I realized a book review I had promised for *Rue Morgue* wasn't going to happen. I simply had too many projects in my lap and wasn't going to be able to read the book in time, let alone review it. In this case, I asked a fellow writer of the magazine if he was willing and able to review the book if I did the introduction. The timing was favorable, and he was able to review the book. So even though I couldn't follow through on my promise, the book still got reviewed by a more than capable writer and got to be published in *Rue Morgue*. The author was happy, and all worked out well because I was timely and honest, and I asked for help.

Speaking of honesty, I feel a guidebook about reviews couldn't be complete if it didn't address what to do if the book turns out to be, well, not good. My own experiences may or may not fit the mold of best practices. It's simply what I've done, and what I continue to do.

Back in about 2018, I acquired a book for review. I read it. And then I sat and pondered what approach my review would take. I mean, there was some truly awe-inspiring prose to be found. Beautiful powerful stuff. Sadly, it was great material that had to be dug out of an overstuffed, rambling jumble of meandering descriptions and action, which was constantly stunted by being over-the-top wordy. What was I supposed to do? I was a fairly new reviewer, and the last thing I wanted to do was piss off an author who no doubt worked his ass off to write his book. I didn't want to be known as "that reviewer" and make anyone nervous to send me their stories to review. On the other hand, I didn't want to be known as a bullshitter whose opinion couldn't be trusted.

In the end, I went with honesty and wrote what I considered to be a fair assessment. While I did mention the outstanding and often brilliant prose, I also mentioned the challenges caused by the overabundance of unnecessary wordage. I did encourage readers to pick up a copy and enjoy it for what it was, but I also warned them that not all of it may be enjoyable. After I polished my review, I did what I always do and I sent a sneak peek of my review to the author. Then I waited for what I was sure to be a pissed off, offended author looking to rip me a new one and correct my ignorant ways regarding his book.

A REVIEWER'S GUIDE TO WRITING BOOK REVIEWS

Instead, I got something else: The author asked me specifically what it was that I felt weighed down the book's prose and why I didn't enjoy it more than I did. Thinking he was being a professional and trying to figure out if my two cents had any value to him, I stuck with the honest approach and told him that the incredible writing was weighed down heavily with run-on, rambling descriptions that often took so long to get where they were headed that the book became more of a burden than it deserved. To my surprise, he replied with agreement and explained how the book was an early draft of the first novel he ever wrote despite having published others first. He felt it was worth getting out to the public and struggled to cut a ton of inflated words out before the version I read was made available. The whole exchange became a learning experience for us both, on top of which I learned that honesty is always the best policy when dealing with opinions about other people's stories. For what it's worth, I went on to read other stories from this author and enjoyed them immensely.

I've also since learned that if I promise to read a book for review and find the book to be something I enjoy very little, I have no issues sending a polite note telling the author that the book isn't quite to my liking and that I will pass on it in hopes it can be more favorably reviewed by a reviewer with different tastes than my own. I consider myself fortunate that I've had very good luck in that most of the books I've read for review have been at least mostly enjoyable, even if from authors I had not previously read before. One of my greatest joys as a reviewer is reading a book by someone I've never heard of before and discovering my new favorite author. And if I read a book that I find to be decent, but also not overly outstanding? I'll be sure to mention my favorite aspects of the book while mentioning a thing or two that didn't quite work well for me. I may mention a book's shortcomings briefly before going on to suggest why others may enjoy it, but I won't dwell on them. For me, it feels like the right and fair thing to do, and most importantly, it's honest without being belligerent or disrespectful in any way to the author or to readers who might end up liking the book more than I did.

I feel like there are probably a few more things of value I could add to this section if given enough time and thought, but honestly? I could just as easily sum it up by saying be professional, don't be an asshole, be considerate, and don't give up. Keep that in mind, and you're good to go. I also don't want to be condescending to you all reading this because I'm pretty sure you have the sense to keep all these things in mind without having to read it from someone like me. That said, the couple of scenarios I mentioned should be enough to give you an idea of some of the situations you may come across and prompt you to consider what you would do as your own best practice. After all, it's always your call. I also feel like for every group of reviewers reading this, there are likely to be at least a few writers among you. At the very least, some of you may have friends who write fiction and are wondering the best way for them to find and interact with reviewers for best results. This leads me to my next and final section of this guidebook.

BONUS ROUND FOR WRITERS

FINDING US, USING US, WORKING WITH US

I WANTED TO ADD this brief bonus section to help inform authors of some best practices to help reviewers better serve them. By including this section, I'm also hoping to make the relationships between authors and reviewers a touch more beneficial for both sides of the fence.

Of all the advice I can suggest for authors, the number one thing is this: It is an absolute Godsend when a reviewer can get as much notice as possible for when your next book is being published. A month or two of advance notice is good. Three, four, or more months' notice is awesome. If the review is going to be written for a blog or online publication, then the biggest hurdle for a reviewer is simply organizing their time so they can read the book, write the review, and send it to its final destination as soon as possible.

However, if the review is going to be pitched to an editor or published in a print publication, then more notice is better. Many print magazines are published on a bi-monthly or quarterly basis and schedule their content two or three months in advance. Generally, book reviews have a shelf life of about two months, with three months being extremely generous, and only then if a magazine really needs some extra space filled at the last minute. If your book comes in December, but you're only letting reviews know about it in November, it's too late for bigger publications. If a reviewer wants to pitch it to a print publication, they won't be able to because that publication is already thinking about their March or May issue. I understand sometimes authors don't get the notice of their book's release until within a couple of months of publication, or their publisher doesn't have ARCs available until shortly before a book's release. The sooner we know you've got a book coming up, the more time we have to pitch and publish our reviews on the best platforms available to us.

If you send us a review copy of your work and we have promised to review the book, don't be afraid to give us a gentle nudge near the time we said we would review the book if a specific time was given. If we get paid anything at all for the time it takes us to review your work, I guarantee it still won't be enough to quit our day jobs. Which is to say we all have lives outside of writing and reading, some busier than others. If you haven't heard back about your review in a reasonable time (based on any promises made or your publication date, whichever comes first), chances are we simply forgot. It happens. It's not intentional, and a friendly reminder/follow-up is generally welcomed and encouraged.

Obviously, if a reviewer promises to review a book at a specific time on a specific platform and doesn't follow through, well, in that case, send 'em to me, and I'll recommend they read the etiquette section of this guide. No promises, though.

ARE WE THERE YET?

CONGRATULATIONS, WE MADE IT! We have reached the end, or rather, as I hope it becomes for you, the beginning of writing well-crafted reviews of books you love and getting paid to do it. It's my goal and my wish that what I have compiled in this guide—the culmination of my twenty years of experience of writing reviews—helps you in some way if not in many ways both expected and unexpected. Did I waste all those years reviewing books when I should have focused on some other hobby instead? I'll let you decide that, but here's hoping at least some of the skills I've learned along the way wind up being of service and support to you, my fellow readers and reviewers. Even if only a few of you reading this now become inspired to craft reviews of your own—whether you get paid for them or are simply writing for the love—then I can consider this guidebook a ridiculous success.

Without a doubt, I'm bound to think of more things I could have added in the coming weeks and months of this guidebook's publication. I'm sure I have forgotten a point or two I should have included—maybe even the point you needed to get just one percent better—but such is the nature of any guide, I suppose. I can already see the likelihood of updating the digital edition of this book. I may need to learn how to do that.

Thank you. Did I forget to say thank you? Thanks to you, dear readers and reviewers. Without your love of reading and sharing your findings with anyone willing to listen, this guidebook would cease to exist, and countless fellow readers may not be discovering their next favorite book or author. Thanks for taking a chance on me and this guide. May it help to enhance whatever you're already doing to share and discuss the books you love with as many readers as possible.

Thanks for being a part of my journey and for allowing me to be a part of yours. Whatever you do, keep reading. Keep sharing that love. And, above all else, stay hungry . . . stay dark.

THE END?

Not if you want to dive into more of Crystal Lake Publishing's Tales from the Darkest Depths!

Check out our amazing website and online store
or download our latest catalog here.
https://geni.us/CLPCatalog

Looking for award-winning Dark Fiction?
Download our latest catalog.

Includes our anthologies, novels, novellas, collections,
poetry, non-fiction, and specialty projects.

WHERE STORIES COME ALIVE!

We always have great new projects and content on the website to dive into, as well as a newsletter, behind the scenes options, social media platforms, our own dark fiction shared-world series and our very own webstore. Our webstore even has categories specifically for KU books, non-fiction, anthologies, and of course more novels and novellas.

ABOUT THE AUTHOR

Rick Hipson is a Canadian writer who loves nothing more than to spend time with his family, prevent his cats from completing full world domination, and soaking up the natural beauty of the great outdoors every moment he can. Otherwise, he can be found devouring every horrific book and movie he can if only to pick the minds of their creators in the hopes of better understanding a chaotic world syphoned through the lenses of those brave enough make art from the fringes of the darkest parts of the human condition.

Hipson has been reviewing, interviewing, and writing articles since around 2004. His recent reviews, interviews and articles have been published in Rue Morgue magazine, Cemetery Dance publications, Apex magazine, Dark Side magazine and his own video podcast, Dark Bites (https://www.youtube.com/channel/UC-AyqqeVx YWboYS33CyfCIQ). He also has a bi-weekly author interview column called What Screams May Come you can find at Cemetery Dance Online.

Visit him on Linktree (https://linktr.ee/rickhipson) and follow him on the socials.

ALSO AVAILABLE BY RICK HIPSON

Dark Bites: Volume 1
A collection of reviews and interviews with upcoming and award-winning creators in dark culture entertainment.

DARKBITES.CA
A video podcast dedicated to conversing with the most exciting up and coming and award-winning horror creators in the industry.

What Screams May Come
A bi-weekly column featuring horror authors and the books they're publishing.

Follow me on Twitter: **@darkbitesblog**
Follow me on Instagram: darkbitesbyrickhipson
Follow me on Tiktok: Dark Bites

Readers . . .

Thank you for reading *A Reviewer's Guide to Writing Book Reviews*. We hope you enjoyed this non-fiction guide.

If you have a moment, please review *A Reviewer's Guide to Writing Book Reviews* at the store where you bought it.

Help other readers by telling them why you enjoyed this book. No need to write an in-depth discussion. Even a single sentence will be greatly appreciated. Reviews go a long way to helping a book sell, and is great for an author's career. It'll also help us to continue publishing quality books.

Thank you again for taking the time to journey with Crystal Lake Publishing.

Visit our Linktree page for a list of our social media platforms. https://linktr.ee/CrystalLakePublishing

Follow us on Amazon:

Our Mission Statement:

Since its founding in August 2012, Crystal Lake Publishing has quickly become one of the world's leading publishers of Dark Fiction and Horror books. In 2023, Crystal Lake Publishing formed a part of Crystal Lake Entertainment, joining several other divisions, including Torrid Waters, Crystal Lake Comics, Crystal Lake Kids, and many more.

While we strive to present only the highest quality fiction and entertainment, we also endeavour to support authors along their writing journey. We offer our time and experience in non-fiction projects, as well as author mentoring and services, at competitive prices.

With several Bram Stoker Award wins and many other wins and nominations (including the HWA's Specialty Press Award), Crystal Lake Publishing puts integrity, honor, and respect at the forefront of our publishing operations.

We strive for each book and outreach program we spearhead to not only entertain and touch or comment on issues that affect our readers, but also to strengthen and support the Dark Fiction field and its authors.

Not only do we find and publish authors we believe are destined for greatness, but we strive to work with men and women who endeavour to be decent human beings who care more for others than themselves, while still being hard working, driven, and passionate artists and storytellers.

Crystal Lake Publishing is and will always be a beacon of what passion and dedication, combined with overwhelming teamwork and respect, can accomplish. We endeavour to know each and every one of our readers, while building personal relationships with our authors, reviewers, bloggers, podcasters, bookstores, and libraries.

We will be as trustworthy, forthright, and transparent as any business can be, while also keeping most of the headaches away from our authors, since it's our job to solve the problems so they can stay in a creative mind. Which of course also means paying our authors.

We do not just publish books, we present to you worlds within your world, doors within your mind, from talented authors who sacrifice so much for a moment of your time.

There are some amazing small presses out there, and through collaboration and open forums we will continue to support other presses in the goal of helping authors and showing the world what quality small presses are capable of accomplishing. No one wins when a small press goes down, so we will always be there to support hardworking, legitimate presses and their authors. We don't see Crystal Lake as the best press out there, but we will always strive to be the best, strive to be the most interactive and grateful, and even blessed press around. No matter what happens over time, we will also take our mission very seriously while appreciating where we are and enjoying the journey.

What do we offer our authors that they can't do for themselves through self-publishing?

We are big supporters of self-publishing (especially hybrid publishing), if done with care, patience, and planning. However, not every author has the time or inclination to do market research, advertise, and set up book launch strategies. Although a lot of authors are successful in doing it all, strong small presses will always be there for the authors who just want to do what they do best: write.

What we offer is experience, industry knowledge, contacts and trust built up over years. And due to our strong brand and trusting fanbase, every Crystal Lake Publishing book comes with weight of respect. In time our fans begin to trust our judgment and will try a new author purely based on our support of said author.

With each launch we strive to fine-tune our approach, learn from our mistakes, and increase our reach. We continue to assure our authors that we're here for them and that we'll carry the weight of the launch and dealing with third parties while they focus on their strengths—be it writing, interviews, blogs, signings, etc.

We also offer several mentoring packages to authors that include knowledge and skills they can use in both traditional and self-publishing endeavours.

We look forward to launching many new careers.

This is what we believe in. What we stand for. This will be our legacy.

Welcome to Crystal Lake Publishing—
Tales from the Darkest Depths.

9 781964 398105